"You've never let me see you like this before," Andres murmured, his hands brushing the sheer silk covering Sarah's body. **"Why now?"**

She didn't have an answer, at least not one she was willing to give. "Don't, Andres, please," she said, but her strength was gone, and he knew she could no longer resist him.

His arms surrounded her, drawing her against him as his mouth found hers. Always before, he'd kept a tight rein on his desire, offering her only gentleness. Now it seemed there was little gentleness in him. His mouth was hot, hard, demanding. He kissed her with all the untamed force of his need, and it left Sara reeling.

It was like a sudden storm blown up out of nowhere, battering her defenses until she felt bruised, bewildered. Yet her arms had somehow wound around his waist and held him with all the strength she could muster. She had to stop this, had to—

"I could take you now, Sara," he said, with eyes that burned even in the night. "And you wouldn't stop me. You wouldn't even try. . . ."

WHAT ARE *LOVESWEPT* ROMANCES?

They are stories of true romance and touching emotion. We believe those two very important ingredients are constants in our highly sensual and very believable stories in the *LOVESWEPT* line. Our goal is to give you, the reader, stories of consistently high quality that may sometimes make you laugh, sometimes make you cry, but are always fresh and creative and contain many delightful surprises within their pages.

Most romance fans read an enormous number of books. Those they truly love, they keep. Others may be traded with friends and soon forgotten. We hope that each *LOVESWEPT* romance will be a treasure—a "keeper." We will always try to publish

LOVE STORIES YOU'LL NEVER FORGET
BY AUTHORS YOU'LL ALWAYS REMEMBER

The Editors

LOVESWEPT® • 286

Kay Hooper
Shades of Gray

BANTAM BOOKS
TORONTO • NEW YORK • LONDON • SYDNEY • AUCKLAND

SHADES OF GRAY
A Bantam Book / October 1988

If you would be interested in receiving protective vinyl
covers for your Loveswept books, please write to this address
for information:

Loveswept
Bantam Books
P.O. Box 985
Hicksville, NY 11802

ISBN 0-553-21905-7

Published simultaneously in the United States and Canada

Bantam Books are published by Bantam Books, a division
of Bantam Doubleday Dell Publishing Group, Inc. Its trademark, consisting of the words "Bantam Books" and the
portrayal of a rooster, is Registered in U.S. Patent and
Trademark Office and in other countries. Marca Registrada.
Bantam Books, 666 Fifth Avenue, New York, New York 10103.

PRINTED IN THE UNITED STATES OF AMERICA

O   0 9 8 7 6 5 4 3 2 1

Prologue

Hagen looked up, honestly surprised for one of the few times in his checkered career. Raven Long had just strolled into his office with the very large and very menacing Zach Steele behind her.

"Hi," she said casually.

Glowering, Hagen responded by demanding, "How did you get into this building?"

Raven shook her head in gentle pity as she settled a hip on the corner of Hagen's desk. "You really should get out more, you know. It's getting awfully easy to catch you off guard."

He ignored that. Splendidly. "I asked you a question."

Smiling, she jerked a thumb over her shoulder at her companion. "Zach's very good at things like that. You said so yourself."

Hagen stared at the big man who was Chief of Security for Long Enterprises and also was quite possibly one of the top three security experts in the world. And since Zach Steele was such an expert, Hagen knew full well how capable he was at breaching other people's security systems—especially when Josh Long or his wife, Raven, former agent, required such a breach.

"Breaching the security of a federal building," Hagen said rather mildly, "is a federal offense, Mr. Steele."

"So it is," Zach agreed in his deep, soft voice, his gray eyes serene.

Hagen sighed. "Well, you're here." He looked at Raven with disfavor. "What do you want?"

She looked over her shoulder at Zach. "He still has the power to amaze me. He ropes innocent citizens into his nefarious plots, unethically, if not illegally, swearing them in as temporary agents and using them shamefully, and he has the nerve, the absolute *gall*, to ask what we want. Amazing."

Hagen didn't rise to the bait. "I'm waiting."

In a wistful tone Zach said to Raven, "One of these days he's going to get what's coming to him. And I want to be there."

Raven sighed an agreement, then returned her gaze to her former boss. Her merry violet eyes became abruptly hard. "Leave Sara Marsh alone," she said gently.

Hagen didn't bat an eye. "I don't know who you're talking about."

"Oh, I think you do. Or has your memory slipped with the passing years? A couple of years ago Sara Marsh left Kadeira and Andres Sereno; a few months after that *you* sent Rafferty and Sarah Lewis down there to get Kelsey out of jail. Remember now?"

Hagen smiled like a shark. "Now that you mention it, I do. But I fail to see—"

"A few weeks ago," Raven went on flatly, interrupting him without compunction, "there was an attempt to kidnap Sara Marsh. Luckily she has good instincts, and managed to slip out while her would-be abductors were slipping in. She was in touch with our Sarah for a while, but in losing your goons, she lost us too. Unfortunately she doesn't know us well enough to trust that we're entirely on her side. But you know that. And just as soon as we manage to locate her, we'll help her to hide where you'll never find her."

Hagen's smile slipped a notch. "That's a serious accusation, Raven," he said sternly.

"Isn't it?" she agreed cordially. "And kidnapping is still, I believe, a federal offense. Even more of an offense in this case because Sara was to be snatched for the express purpose of transporting her to Kadeira, which is the last place on earth she would choose to be, as her past actions amply demonstrate. Now she's being hunted. Since when have agents of the U.S. government decided to kidnap citizens on the orders of Andres Sereno? Or have you taken up pimping these days?"

It was an uncharacteristically harsh question coming from Raven, and Hagen's smile faded entirely. His pink Cupid's face hardened, and his pouty lips firmed into a straight line. After a long moment he said irritably, "You're being naïve. And while we're on the subject, just what right did you and your colleagues have to help Derek Ross enrage an unstable Middle Eastern dictator a few weeks ago?"

Without hesitation she said, "The right as citizens to fight traitors. Now let's hear your answer."

He met her gaze solidly. "I, Mrs. Long, have the right and the duty as a government agent to exercise those powers granted to me by my commander in chief."

"Lot of that going around these days," Zach murmured.

Raven made a rude sound. "Let's cut to the chase, shall we? Sereno couldn't find Sara, so he called in a favor from you. And now you're planning to send her to Kadeira, even though she doesn't want to go."

"Someone else," Hagen said, "owes President Sereno a favor, if I recall correctly."

Readily she said, "Josh does. But you'll notice Sereno didn't ask Josh to kidnap Sara—because he knew that favor would be refused. Instead he asked you. And we all know you're capable of anything."

"You're out of line," Hagen said in a stony voice.

"So are you! We fought for years, you and I, to break white slavery rings; what in the name of hell do you think *this* is? She doesn't want to go back there, Hagen, and if that man really loved her, he wouldn't try to force her." Raven drew a deep breath. "So we're here to warn you. If we find out Sara Marsh has been taken to Kadeira against her will, we'll break the story to the press and get it worldwide coverage."

"I wouldn't do that if I were you," Hagen said mildly enough. "A new extradition treaty with Kadeira is about to be announced. It is perfectly legal to extradite criminals."

Raven slid off the desk and straightened up

slowly. Her face was still, her eyes cold. "You bastard."

He smiled.

"That poor girl never broke a law in her life— not here, and not on Kadeira!" Raven snapped.

"It's on the record," Hagen said. Or will be by the time anyone checks, he amended silently.

Without another word Raven swung around and strode from the office with Zach. And Hagen barely caught her fierce statement to the big man.

"We've got to find Sara before *he* does."

Hagen looked at the brass ashtray on his desk, which contained a tiny pile of ashes; he had burned a message slip just before his visitors had arrived. "Too late," he murmured to himself. And then, to the empty office, he made a statement that none of his staff, past or present, would have believed.

"I've made a mistake."

One

She was too angry to be afraid. The injection
they'd given her had acted quickly, and she was
hardly surprised to awaken in the small cabin of a
boat. She held her aching head with one hand
and sat up on the bunk, gazing out the porthole
at the open sea. That also didn't surprise her. It
was sometime around mid-afternoon, she guessed.
The day after the afternoon they'd shanghaied
her. She'd slept a long time.

And she didn't have to look at a map to know
that she was somewhere off the northern coast of
South America.

They hadn't hurt her. In fact, her kidnappers
had sustained considerable damage themselves
from her struggles, because they'd been taking
great pains not to hurt her. And she understood
why, of course.

Andres would have them shot if they harmed
her.

The cabin was small, but there was enough room to stretch the kinks from her legs. On a small table near the bunk she discovered a tray covered with a linen napkin, under which reposed an appetizing meal of cold chicken and salad. She ignored the food but poured a glass of wine from the carafe and sipped it.

Pacing the restricted floor space absently, she stretched aching muscles and automatically straightened her clothing—snug, faded blue jeans and a casual summer blouse the same color as her eyes.

As the last of the cobwebs cleared from her mind, she sighed and opened the door, unsurprised to find that it wasn't locked. Where, after all, could she escape to? She went up the steps and onto the deck, squinting into the bright sunlight.

"Good afternoon, miss."

She looked at the man who had spoken. He was a lean, hard man somewhere in his thirties, with soulful eyes and a rather chillingly gentle smile. She didn't know him.

"Hello." Somewhat mockingly she saluted him with her wineglass.

"The food—"

"I wasn't hungry."

He half bowed, oddly graceful. "I am the captain, miss."

She nodded. "When will we arrive?"

"In a few hours."

After a long silence she sighed. "I don't suppose," she said, "there's a boat I could steal to make good my escape?"

He blinked. "No, miss."

"And I also don't suppose it would be at all wise of me to jump overboard and try swimming for it?"

"No, miss."

"Then don't bother to hover over me, Captain," she said, and turned away to walk toward the bow.

Siran grimaced faintly, half in admiration and half in doubt. An interesting woman, his passenger. The men who had brought her to the ship off Trinidad had borne ample proof of her ability to defend herself, yet she seemed perfectly calm now. He watched her critically for a moment.

She was a tiny woman, barely five feet tall if that, dressed casually in jeans, a green blouse, and running shoes. And though another woman would have probably called her petite, no man worth his salt would have missed the surprisingly lush curves of breasts and hips, guaranteed to stop traffic and haunt dreams.

Her hair was that rare, striking color between red and gold, and it hung thick and shining to the middle of her back. It was styled simply in a layered cut from a center part, and that silky, burnished hair framed a face that was almost too delicately perfect to be real. She was like a painting; every feature was finely drawn with artistic excellence, from her straight nose to the sweet curve of her lips. And in that strikingly perfect face, her eyes were simply incredible: a clear, pale green; huge and shadowed by long, thick lashes.

Siran remembered another woman on a yacht under his command, a woman so like this one that they could have been twins. From what he had seen and heard, that woman had found love on her trips to Kadeira. What would this woman find?

She didn't hear him leave over the noises of wind, ocean, and engine, yet she knew when the captain had finally left her alone. An unsettling man, she thought vaguely. She didn't fear being alone with him on the small boat and felt a flicker of emotion that was a painful inner laugh when she came to this realization. There wasn't much about Andres Sereno of which she could be certain —except the fact that anyone in his employ knew only too well that she had to be kept safe. So she was. A bird in a gilded cage. No, not that, not really. Kadeira was a beautiful island but war-torn. And Sereno, though a powerful man, had chosen to build his country rather than his own personal wealth. The "palace" was a large, comfortable house, but there was nothing gilded about it.

She stood there at the bow, face into the wind, trying not to think. Trying not to remember.

But when the island first came into view, she was surprised by the surge of emotion she felt, and unnerved by the flood of memories that came to mind. It was such a beautiful island, especially from a distance—before the underlying rot became visible.

She flung the empty wineglass overboard with a stifled cry, then gripped the brass railing hard as she stiffened her shoulders and began dragging all the emotions into the dark room where she'd placed them more than two years ago. By the time the harbor came into view, she was calm again.

Not much had changed in two years, she thought. Not, at least, at first glance. It was a good harbor with plenty of room for the score of vessels riding at anchor and tied up to the dock. Except for a few fishing boats, all were military vessels, and all were armed to the teeth.

A cluster of buildings, mostly warehouses, stood near the dock. Off to the left was the striking vista of towering mountains and rolling hills that helped to make the island so beautiful, and off to the right, whitewashed and shining in the bright sunlight, was the island's only real city, and the home of most of its people.

No building rose more than five stories, and all the bright whitewash couldn't hide the scars of a country in turmoil. There was some construction going on but not much, and shorn buildings showed like broken teeth in the rubble of the bombed remains of cars, trucks, and buildings.

She swallowed hard, still fighting for emotional control. Nothing had changed, not really. She had kept up with news reports almost against her will, and knew that the "rebels" still came down from the hills and raided periodically, making it impossible for Sereno to put his economic development plans into effect. Kadeira was a torn country, a wound bleeding its life away.

Soldiers on the docks slung their rifles over their shoulders long enough to tie up the boat, and she paused only a moment to once more give the captain a mocking salute before jumping onto the dock. Ignoring the soldiers, she walked steadily forward to greet the slender man with a military carriage who was waiting for her near a long black limo.

"Colonel," she said briefly.

"Miss Marsh." Expressionless, he held the door for her.

She got into the car and looked steadily out the window during the ride, saying nothing more to Colonel Durant. She had liked him once, but she was afraid to let herself feel anything right now. They drove by the old presidential palace, now a hospital. And if she winced at the evidence of recent fighting—buildings she remembered as relatively intact were now in rubble—at least it was inwardly.

The limo passed through the guarded gates and wound its way up the drive to the plain stucco two-storied house. As she got out of the car she saw that the flowers she'd planted in window boxes were still alive and obviously cared for. But the bars on the windows, ornate though they were, were still visible, still a grim testament to their purpose—like the soldiers who constantly patrolled the grounds.

She followed Colonel Durant into the house, steeling herself against her memories. When he silently indicated that she should wait in the book-lined room she had once loved, she went in with gritted teeth.

The memories . . . She went to the French doors and stared out into the garden, her cold hands in the pockets of her jeans, her back stiff. Oh, Lord, the memories!

"Sara?"

She didn't move, didn't say a word. Her eyes closed and she swallowed hard. For a long moment she stood with her back to him, wondering dimly how many times she had heard his voice say her name—in her dreams.

Sara Marsh moved slowly, bracing herself even more as she turned to face him. He hadn't changed much in two years. He was unusual among his countrymen in that he was over six feet tall and powerfully built. He was dressed casually in dark slacks and a white shirt unbuttoned at the throat beneath an open jacket, but the informal attire did nothing to conceal the physical strength of broad shoulders and powerful limbs, or the honed grace of his movements when he stepped toward her. He was dark, black-haired, and black-eyed, his lean face handsome and bearing none of the outward marks or scars of his reportedly difficult and violent life.

Perhaps he was a shade leaner, the planes and angles of his face sharper, his eyes more deeply hooded. And there were, she saw with a curious pang, a few strands of silver among the ebony at his temples.

And she knew, then, that she had forgotten nothing. Nothing at all.

He was Andres Sereno, President of the island country of Kadeira, commander in chief of its army and navy, both titles earned by sweat and blood and viewed askance by an American government that had never been quite sure if he was enemy, friend, or merely neutral. He had been called a dictator—and worse.

"Hello, Andres." Her voice emerged cool and calm, and she thanked the fates for control.

He took another step toward her, and the quiet, innately powerful voice that had moved the people of his country was a little rough. a little husky. "You're as beautiful as I remembered."

Sara inclined her head politely.

His face tightened a little. "Sara, I know you're angry with me, but I—I had to bring you here."

"I'm here. I had no choice in the matter. But then, I should have known my wishes didn't mean a damned thing to you. I made it clear two years ago that I never wanted to see you again, yet I've been on the run ever since in order to stay one jump ahead of your hounds."

He shoved his hands into his pockets suddenly, matching her stance as they confronted each other. "Am I allowed no defense? No opportunity to explain my actions? I needed to see you, Sara. I didn't want to do this, but you gave me no choice."

Sara didn't have to fake scorn. "Oh, it's all my fault that I was kidnapped? Was I supposed to just tamely submit to your paid goons and come along like a good little girl?"

"They didn't hurt you?" he asked swiftly.

"No," she said flatly.

Andres relaxed almost imperceptibly. "Sara, I tried to respect your wishes. And I would have, if only you hadn't vanished so completely. The letters I sent to your sister's home were returned unopened. When I called, she refused to tell me where you were. What else could I do?"

"You could have left me alone!" she said fiercely.

"No, Sara, I couldn't." Softly he added, "Because I love you."

It shook her now as it had shaken her in the past, and Sara wondered wildly how a man so shut in and as remote as Andres could make that declaration so easily—and so convincingly. He was charming and charismatic, but there was a large room surrounding the core of himself marked KEEP OUT, and that was the part of him she was afraid of.

She drew a deep breath. "I don't care." She did, but that was something he could never know. "Whatever I might have felt for you died the day I found out those terrorists were on Kadeira."

"They're gone now," he told her.

"And that makes everything all right?" She could feel all her muscles tensing, and her stomach churning sickly when she thought of the terrorists. "Let me go, Andres."

"I can't."

Sara was aware of an inner tremor, and knew that her control was right on the edge, faltering. She didn't know how much more of this she could take. "Do you know what my life's been like for the past two years?" she asked steadily.

"Sara—"

"It's been hell. I've developed the instincts of a hunted animal. I can't walk down a street without searching every face, tensing at every sound. I can't have a home, because it's a lot easier and quicker to run from a hotel or a lousy apartment. I can't have friends, because I don't know who to trust. I haven't been able to do a damned thing with my life, and if I didn't happen to have income from my parents' estate, I wouldn't even have been able to live, except from hand to mouth, because I can't hold down a job! Is that what you wanted, Andres? Is that how you meant to punish me for leaving you?"

His face was white, his eyes bottomless. After a moment he turned and moved a few feet away before turning back to face her. His smile was twisted. "You could always make me feel things I didn't want to feel. That hasn't changed."

She wanted to cry. "Let me go."

He shook his head a little and said, "I have a proposition for you."

Sara waited, tense and afraid.

"A month. Remain on Kadeira for a month. If, after that, you wish to leave, then I'll see that you're taken back to the States." His voice was even. "And I'll give you my word of honor that I'll never interfere in your life again."

The silence was long as Sara tried to figure out what he was up to. "What do you expect to happen in a month?"

"I want . . ." He hesitated, then finished roughly, "I want the time with you, that's all. Is it so difficult for you to understand?"

"You want me to stay here, in your home?"

He sighed. "It's safer, you know that. Of course, you'll have your own suite of rooms."

Two years ago he hadn't tried to take advantage of her confusion, hadn't insisted on a physical relationship even though the attraction had been explosive; she wasn't sure about his attitude now. "And if I—I refuse your proposition?"

Andres seemed to brace himself. "I can't let you go."

She laughed shortly. "I don't seem to have a choice—again."

"You have a choice," he said quietly.

Sara knew what he was saying. "All right, then. I'll stay for a month. It's a small enough price to pay to be free of you for good." The final sentence was harsh, and she regretted the words even before Andres winced.

"I don't want you hurt," he said softly. "Just try to remember that, Sara."

She nodded, not trusting her voice. And she couldn't apologize for hurting him, because she couldn't let him know that his feelings mattered to her.

"The suite that was yours before has been prepared for you," he said formally. "The things you left are still here. If there are any other things you need, Maria will get them for you."

"Thank you." Sara kept her own voice formal. "If you don't mind, I'll go up to my rooms now. Is dinner at the same time?"

"Yes."

Sara escaped, her heart thudding and her eyes burning. She found that she remembered the way, up the curved staircase and along the open hall to the third door on the right. Andres's rooms were at the end of the hall.

She went into the sitting room, looking around to find that nothing had changed. The suite was light and airy, the colors pastels, the furniture comfortable. Her portable tape player and box of cassettes were on the small desk, just where she'd left them, and she had no doubt there would be fresh batteries. In the bedroom, the closet and dresser drawers still contained the clothing she'd left behind, carefully cleaned and neatly preserved.

She had been living in Trinidad for the winter when they had met, and so had most of her possessions with her. And when she had bolted from Kadeira in sick despair, all her things had been left behind. He had, she saw, kept everything, as if he had been confident she would return.

Sara wandered into the bathroom, unsurprised to find her favorite scents in soaps and bath oils. She wanted to cry again. She quickly stripped for a shower and stepped underneath the warm water, letting it wash away her tears.

Durant entered the library quietly, unsurprised to find Sereno standing at the French doors and gazing out into the garden. With the license allowed an old and trusted friend, he asked, "How did it go?"

Sereno laughed, a low sound that held no amusement. He didn't turn around. "Much as I expected. She hates me, Vincente."

"The terrorists still?"

"That—and the past two years."

Durant frowned at the strong, still back of his president. "I don't understand."

"They hounded her. She hasn't had a moment's peace since she left here."

"But when you told her—"

"I didn't. Nothing will change her hate for me, and I don't want her to be afraid. It doesn't matter." He sighed. "We have a month to do what we must. I can't keep her here against her will longer than that."

"Andres—"

"Does Lucio know yet?" Sereno asked, interrupting.

"Undoubtedly. He has spies in the town, watching the harbor. Someone is sure to have reported her arrival. Andres, a month isn't enough time.

After all these years Lucio knows the island like a wolf knows his lair. He's cunning, and he won't give up now that Sara is back; she's close enough to be too tempting to him."

"I know." Sereno finally turned to face his friend, and his smile was twisted. "But here, at least, I can protect her. Double the guard around the perimeter, Vincente. I want the best possible security here at the house, and Sara is not to leave the grounds."

Durant nodded. "Of course. And Lucio?"

Sereno shook his head a little. "We wait for him to move. I don't dare weaken security here by ordering the men into the hills to look for him."

"If only—" Durant broke off, frowning.

"Yes. If only. If only we had more men, better equipment." Sereno laughed, again without amusement, and this time with faint bitterness. "I command a splendid navy, Vincente, and what good does it do me? Lucio fights on the land. And as long as his forces and mine are equally armed, it will remain a stalemate. I've used all the tricks I know, old friend."

"Not all of them," Durant said steadily.

After a moment Sereno nodded. "Yes, Long owes me a favor. And what am I to ask, Vincente? Money for arms? He doesn't deal in guns. Should I ask him again to invest here in my country? What business would survive? How many times have we tried to rebuild, only to see our efforts destroyed in the night by Lucio's canny harassment?"

"There must be a way," Durant said flatly. "You've struggled for too many years, Andres. You've sacrificed too much. There must be a way to win!" He drew a deep breath, then said, "Lucio must be destroyed before he destroys you."

Sereno turned back to gaze out the French doors again. "Yes. Don't worry, old friend. He hasn't beaten me yet."

Durant left the library silently. He wasn't worried that Sereno might have given up; defeat had never been a viable option for Andres Sereno, and never would. Not, at least, where his country's future was concerned. But Durant knew only too well that despair of another kind could bow the shoulders of a strong man—especially a strong man.

And Sara didn't know the truth.

It was a couple of hours later when Sara ventured from her rooms. Downstairs, the door to Andres's office was closed, and she passed it silently. She found Maria in the kitchen, and the housekeeper welcomed her warmly and insisted on preparing her a cup of the tea she loved.

"It's good you're back," she told Sara, nodding decisively, her bright brown eyes smiling. "The house has been so quiet and empty. So has he."

Sara refused to be moved by the simple comment. "I'm just here for a visit, Maria," she said easily. "A few weeks."

"Much can happen in weeks."

Unsettled by the comment, Sara agreed silently. Much *could* happen in weeks. It had before. Within the space of a few weeks her entire life had changed. She had met Andres, been fascinated and charmed, swept off her feet by his intense courtship, even to the point of coming here to stay at his home. And then, with dreadful suddenness, she had learned of the terrorists and, sickened by their presence and Andres's acceptance of them, had run blindly. And had been running ever since.

Sara drew a breath and set her empty cup aside. "I think I'll go walk in the garden," she told the housekeeper.

Maria nodded agreeably but said, cautioning, "Stay on the grounds. It's not safe to wander alone."

Thinking of the tall fence surrounding the grounds, Sara wondered if she would be allowed outside. She went into the garden, seeing here and there a shrub or a flower that she remembered suggesting to the old gardener, Carlos. There were even the roses she loved, scores of them in all varieties, planted neatly in beautiful beds, though there had been none in the garden two years ago. All around her she saw her own presence, her own influence; in the few short weeks of her stay here it seemed she had left footprints of a sort.

But the largest footprint she had left caught her by surprise, and she stood in the bend of the path, staring in wonder at the delicate little gazebo.

Her own words came back to her: "Such a beautiful view of the mountains here, Andres. You should build a gazebo, a place where you can come and just sit peacefully. A place to rest. You need a place to rest."

Sara half closed her eyes, hurting.

"Miss Marsh?"

She walked forward toward the gazebo but spoke to the man behind her. "You called me Sara before, Colonel."

"And you called me Vincente," Durant reminded her, following.

Sara stood inside the gazebo just gazing at the mountains for a moment, then sat down on the cushioned seat of a wrought-iron chair. "So I did. Were you looking for me, Vincente?"

He stood, militarily erect as always, and his thin face was hard. "I was. I wanted to talk to you."

She looked up at him curiously, aware of his tension. "Well, you have a—a captive audience," she said wryly.

His face seemed to harden even more. "I wanted to ask what happened to the woman who planted flowers in window boxes? What happened to the woman who loved roses and yet never waited for those Andres had ordered to arrive? The woman who brightened the house with her laughter. I wanted to ask, Sara, what happened to the woman Andres loved?"

"What happened to her?" Sara felt cold. "I'll tell you what happened to her. Somebody yanked away her rose-colored glasses, that's what happened. She found out she wasn't living in a fairy tale complete with a happily-ever-after ending." Sara drew a deep breath. "They were *terrorists*, Vincente, killing innocent people, men and women and children, murdering in wholesale lots, and Andres *condoned* it!"

"He never condoned it," Durant said quietly.

"He let them have sanctuary."

"There were reasons."

Sara laughed shortly. "Of course. They paid him money to live here, didn't they, Vincente? And Kadeira needs money. But I suppose that isn't surprising, that Andres would choose to fill his coffers with blood money. Variations of that have kept Kadeira a flourishing seat of revolution for fifty years."

"You don't understand anything," Durant told her. "You didn't grow up here, didn't go hungry as a child—"

"And Andres did. Yes, I know that." She kept her voice as cold as possible, unwilling to be moved. "Still, it doesn't justify what he did. Nothing justifies the acceptance of terrorists."

"You never asked him why, did you, Sara? You just ran in the night, tearing the heart out of him—"

"And I've been running ever since!" she said, interrupting fiercely. "Hunted like an animal until he finally caught me. So don't expect any sympathy, *Colonel* Durant!"

There was a moment of silence, and then Durant said wearily, "He should have told you. Perhaps he would have, but you looked at him as though he were a monster, didn't you, Sara? Your mind was made up, and he was found guilty and convicted by you without even the opportunity to defend himself. You wouldn't have heard him, wouldn't have believed him."

"What are you talking about?"

Durant hesitated, glancing toward the house. Then he sighed. Looking back at her, he said evenly, "Andres has enemies, you know that. The rebel leader, for one."

Impatiently she said, "I know. Lucio."

"Andres and Lucio were once friends. In fact, Lucio was Andres's second in command in the revolution that deposed the former regime. Once

Andres was in power, Lucio became . . . dissatis-
fied, bitter, resentful. Andres was forced to pro-
ceed with caution in his efforts to improve the
country; perhaps Lucio felt he wasn't moving fast
enough. I don't know the full story. I only know
that there was a final, bitter confrontation, and
Lucio fled to the hills and gathered an army. For
several years now he has attempted to destroy
Andres."

"I don't see what that has to do with me," she
said.

Durant smiled bleakly. "Everything. The international press enjoyed their stories of a ruthless
dictator falling in love with a young woman he
had met in Trinidad. Within a matter of days
everyone who could read knew the stories. You
became a possible tool, Sara, for Andres's enemies to use."

After a moment she said slowly, "I don't understand."

"I think you do. One of the reasons Andres
brought you here so soon after you met was to
protect you. Once Lucio learned of Andres's feelings for you, he learned also of the first chink in
Andres's armor. He could have captured you, used
you to bend Andres to his will. When you ran
away, Andres was half mad with fear for you."

"I was safe in the States," she objected.

"No. You were never running from Andres's de-
tectives, Sara; we were never able to get that close.
It was Lucio's confederates who hounded you all
this time. It was they who gave you no peace. If
Andres had not called in a favor from an American agent with far greater resources than our
own, Lucio may well have captured you. Andres

had you *kidnapped* and brought back here so that he could keep you safe."

Sara couldn't believe it, refused to believe it. "I'm only staying a month. Then I have Andres's word that I can go home for good."

Durant nodded. "Yes. It gives us only a few weeks to accomplish what we have been unable to accomplish in years: to defeat the rebels. You will never be safe until Lucio is dead. He knows Andres too well."

Holding on to her precarious disbelief, she said, "It doesn't make sense! It's been two years. Lucio can't possibly think I can be used against Andres now—"

"He's hounded you for two years."

"I only have your word for that!" she snapped.

"You still don't understand, do you?" Durant said harshly. "With you in his hands, Lucio would have anything and everything Andres could give him. You are Andres's one vulnerability. Two years or twenty, it makes no difference. He would sell his very soul to spare you pain! And you looked at him as though he were a *monster.* Think about that."

Two

Long after Durant had stalked back toward the house, Sara stared at the spot where he had stood. "There are still the terrorists," she murmured to herself, but the words were hollow.

The thought was hollow. If it had indeed been Lucio, rather than Andres, who had hounded her for two years . . . if Andres had brought her back here now only to keep her safe until he could deal with Lucio . . .

It wasn't Sara's intention to wait in the garden for Andres to come to her. If she had ever considered that he *would* come to her, she would have believed it unlikely after the things she had said to him. She meant to go to him, to ask him for the truth. But as she sat there in the peaceful gazebo trying to get up her courage, Andres did come.

He came with a guarded face and shuttered eyes, and his voice was calm and formal. "Vincente shouldn't have told you," he said, sitting down in the other chair. "There was no reason to disturb you with Lucio's mad schemes."

"I had a right to know the truth." Her voice was strained. "You should have told me. Would you prefer that I hate you for something you didn't do?"

"Does the reason for the hate matter?" he asked bleakly.

"I don't hate you." She heard the words emerge from her mouth and rose jerkily to go and stand at the railing, staring blindly toward the mountains. *What had she said?* Her control was slipping, and she grasped at it desperately. She knew Andres had gotten to his feet, because he wouldn't sit while a woman stood. She knew he was behind her. "I just can't understand . . ."

"Sara."

She didn't move, didn't turn. No wonder his voice had moved a country already long sick of revolution and suspicious of promises to take up arms and fight yet another war. How easily it moved her, even now. And she was suspicious of promises too. She didn't want to fight. "Do you know how my parents died?" she asked abruptly, her voice uneven.

"No. You never told me."

Sara turned stiffly and faced him, her arms folded protectively, warning him off. "Terrorists."

Andres closed his eyes briefly, and his face tightened. "I'm sorry, Sara."

"They were in Europe. Just . . . coming out of a restaurant. It was their anniversary, you see; and they'd been celebrating. When the bomb went off, it shattered windows for a block. And there wasn't much left of the restaurant. Fifty people died, including my parents. Including a young mother and her baby who were strolling along the sidewalk. All dead. And do you know who claimed responsibility for the explosion?"

He knew. And he now knew why she had run away from him in such anguish. "The Final Legion?"

Sara nodded. "The Final Legion. Such a grand-sounding name, isn't it? Such a grand name for a pack of soulless murderers. They claimed responsibility, grabbing every headline they could, railing against a corrupt society. And they congratulated themselves on their strike for freedom. Then they just melted away . . . laughing." She caught her breath raggedly and lifted her chin, staring at him from hot, hurting eyes. "Six months later I came to Kadeira with a charming man and found out that he allowed them to live here. Knowing—*knowing*—what they were, he gave them a home."

"*Dios*, Sara, I'm so sorry." He stepped toward her, his hands lifting to hold her shoulders gently. "I never wanted to hurt you that way—"

"Is there another way?" she asked fiercely, jerking back from him and moving to put a safe distance between them. She didn't want him to touch her, because when he did, she thought she could mindlessly forgive him worse than terrorists, and that realization terrified her.

Andres slid his hands into his pockets and met her gaze steadily. "What would you have me say? I can't turn back the clock, Sara. I can't tell you they were never here. They *were* here, and I *did* allow them to stay."

"Why? *Why?*" Baffled, she shook her head helplessly. "Because they paid you money? What kind of man does that make you, Andres?"

He stood looking at her for a long moment with something almost hesitant in his eyes. And then, in a change that was as visible to her as a curtain dropping, he was shut inside himself. And she was implacably shut out.

"If you don't know what kind of man I am, Sara," he said remotely, "then nothing I could say would give you that knowledge. But I will tell you this: If I could turn back the clock, I would change only one thing. I would make very certain that you learned of the Final Legion's presence in Kadeira from me, and not from someone else."

"Only that?" she whispered.

"Only that. I would change nothing else. And I will not apologize for my actions, Sara, because I do not regret them. Do you understand? Given the identical situation, I would act now as I acted then."

The unequivocal statement should have made Sara at least more certain of her feelings. His own words, after all, were clear proof that she had been right to escape a man who could welcome terrorists and give them sanctuary in his country, accept payment for his hospitality from them, and then feel no compunction about what he had done two years later. But, oddly, his words only caused her to become even more confused.

It just wasn't *right* that Andres could do such a thing. And yet he had. He didn't deny it. He made no excuses, offered no defense. In fact, his own words were a self-indictment. Yet Sara felt as if he were showing her an image that was somehow distorted, blurred; there was something wrong with the image, and she didn't know what it was. Despite everything, she couldn't quite believe he was as villainous as he seemed. But she didn't trust even that mental wavering. There was still, in Sara, that young woman who had fallen in love with a complex, charismatic man—and had learned, at a high cost to herself, that her own judgment was tragically faulty.

What was he? *What was he?*

"I don't understand," she said finally, hurting too much not to try to make sense of it all.

"No, you don't." Andres's almost gentle voice was in stark contrast to the stonelike expression on his face. "Because I am not playing the game according to the rules, am I? I should apologize, tell you it was all a mistake. That I was wrong to do what I did. You could forgive me for a mistake. Those are the rules. But this isn't a game.

"You want things simple, Sara. Either I am as black as I am painted—or I am not. But the truth is never simple. You could forgive me were I to convince you that I feel regret or remorse for what I did. You could forgive me, and perhaps we could build on that, you and I. But we would build on a lie, and I'll have no lies between us."

Unsteadily she said, "What are you asking of me? That I trust you blindly, accept on faith that you had a good reason to allow them here? To receive money from them? What *reason* could there possibly be, Andres?"

"I did what I had to do," he answered flatly. "The reasons aren't important now. I gave them sanctuary. I won't apologize for that, Sara. Not even to you."

After a moment she turned and walked away from him.

"Well?" Lucio snapped out the question, frowning in annoyance at the sputtering lamp that barely illuminated the dank, dark cave.

His lieutenant, a burly, bearded man named Sabin, sketched a brief, somewhat haphazard salute and reported stolidly, "She's here. A small boat delivered her just a few hours ago. Impossible to get near her; Sereno had a cordon thrown up around the town, and snipers on the rooftops. He was taking no chances."

Lucio leaned back in his chair, his frown deepening. But there was neither surprise nor displeasure in his voice. "I always suspected Andres knew well how to guard a treasure," he remarked. "Particularly if that treasure was coveted by another."

Sabin waited in silence, having learned, like all Lucio's men, that their leader strongly disliked having his thoughts interrupted. In the flickering lamplight Lucio appeared both cruel and intelligent; in his case, appearances were not deceptive. His black eyes, unusually—and perhaps unnaturally—large and brilliant, were filled with cunning. His mouth, wide and mobile, was both sensual and cruel.

He was shrewd in military matters, and commanded loyalty from his men by the sheer strength of his personality—and by fear. They were all afraid of him, Sabin included. But Sabin, like the other lieutenants who formed a barrier between Lucio and his army, was a man who knew nothing but war. When Sereno and Lucio had ended the last revolution and thus brought peace, men like Sabin had been left rudderless.

Eventually, of course, most of those soldiers would have fit themselves into a peacetime military. But in the interim they had been vulnerable, and Lucio's swift defection from Sereno's regime had given Sabin and those like him a new war. Politics mattered not at all to them, only fighting. Lucio had offered a fight, and they had joined him.

And now, waiting patiently, Sabin felt little curiosity about his leader's reasons for wanting the woman. It would be, no doubt, because she could be used as a weapon in some way.

"Andres will see to it that she keeps to the grounds, where he can protect her," Lucio said, musing. "It would be foolish to storm his little fortress, of course. So we shall have to draw the woman out." He glanced up, saw Sabin waiting patiently, and gestured. "We will discuss it later. Dismissed."

Sabin saluted again and left the cave.

Alone, Lucio absently watched the lamplight throw weird shadows on the rough walls. He could hear, out in the cloying heat and damp of their jungle camp, the voices of his men; he didn't think about them. He thought about the woman— and about Andres.

The one could be used to break the other. Once in his possession, the woman would be the most powerful weapon he could hope to use against his bitter enemy. He hadn't decided how best to use that weapon, but he would. Like all his weapons, she would be used to maximum effect.

He meant to destroy Andres Sereno.

"What kind of man does that make you?"

The question echoed in his mind long after Sara had disappeared back toward the house. He stood gazing at the beautiful mountains that not even half a century of revolution had been able to destroy, and he couldn't find an answer to her question.

Did the end justify the means? Did it matter at all that he had allowed them here so they could have been closely observed by the people who intended to bring them to justice? Would Sara understand if he explained that he had been asked by the head of a secret American agency to provide a base for the terrorists just so that they *could* be observed and studied, their weaknesses pinpointed—their next target identified?

Perhaps she would understand. Certainly she would forgive him, he thought. And yet he had been unable to offer that simple explanation. It *was* simple and factual, but it was not the entire truth. It was, as he had told her, far more complex than that. It was a matter of favors asked and owed, a matter of desperate need for his country, a matter of a delicate and dangerous chess game where people named as friends were in fact enemies, where people named as enemies were often friends.

In the end it had been a matter of his own conscience.

He had not sold them arms or offered aid, merely a base where they could live unmolested. He had helped make their continued existence possible, when he just as easily could have ordered his army to capture them. He could have had them executed or had them thrown into his prison for the duration of their natural lives, actions that most of the world no doubt would have applauded privately, if not publicly.

Instead he had offered them sanctuary here on Kadeira—in the eyes of the world. In Sara's eyes. And there had been no connection made by the world or by her when the Final Legion had been quietly and effeciently captured one week after leaving Kadeira, and before they could kill again.

Only Adrian, the leader of that group, had managed to escape, and he hadn't been heard of since. The Final Legion had been more or less forgotten in the year since their capture, replaced in the news by other groups. Forgotten by all except those like Sara, who had lost loved ones.

And by Andres Sereno. He would go to his grave with the blood of their crimes on his soul. But Andres could bear that. He didn't know if Sara could.

He left the gazebo, walking slowly back through the garden, his hands in his pockets. He wondered grimly if he would be able to sit across from her at dinner without disgracing himself; his hands always seemed to shake when he was near her.

She was so lovely . . . and so vitally important to him. And though he had learned to cope easily with foreign governments, with powerful men and enemies, coping with his love for Sara was still the most difficult task of his life. He could be nothing except what he was, and what he was unsettled and frightened her. He knew that. He had seen that even two years ago, even before the Final Legion had driven her away from him.

And because of all that he had never pressed her unfairly, had never taken advantage of the explosive passion between them. Because he had known that if they'd become lovers while some part of her feared him, it could have destroyed them both.

It might still destroy them.

High above the noise of New York City, in a large and luxurious penthouse office, only one voice disturbed the tranquillity of a Wednesday afternoon.

"Hagen," Raven Long said with a rare note of anger in her musical voice, "has lived too long. I always knew that one day he'd do something unforgivable. Well, he's done it. The guys should never have stopped you from killing him, Josh." She was pacing restlessly.

"Oh, I don't know," her husband responded in an absent tone as he bent over a large map on his huge desk. "If they'd let me kill him back then, we probably wouldn't have Sarah, Teddy, or Kyle. Kelsey might have had to look for a new job, which means he probably wouldn't have met Elizabeth. I imagine Derek would have gotten Shannon without Hagen's—or our—help, but you never really know about these things."

On the other side of the desk, Raven bent down to rest on her elbows, but she was looking at Josh rather than the map, and she was smiling. "Guess you're right. Have I told you lately what an excellent husband you turned out to be?"

He looked up from his work, his normally rather hard blue eyes softening when they rested on her face. With a faint grin he asked, "What brought that on?"

Solemnly she said, "Well, you're being very patient with me. You've let me rant and rave and get it all out of my system. That's a rare quality in a husband—and much appreciated."

Josh chuckled but said in a grave tone, "You don't rant and rave very often, darling. And never without reason."

Raven, her reason brought back to mind, sighed. "Seriously, we are going to have to do something about Hagen, and soon. He's been let run wild too long." She shook off wistful thoughts. "First things first, though."

"Meaning Sara Marsh." Josh nodded. "I think you alerted the *Corsair* in time; they were sailing just off Trinidad, so their radar took in Kadeira."

"That's some boat you've got, friend," a new voice interjected.

"Kelsey, did you find Derek?" Raven asked, frowning down at the map.

"I've been out of touch, you know," Raven's ex-partner said in a wounded tone as he approached them.

She looked up at him, one eyebrow rising sardonically.

Kelsey grinned. "As a matter of fact, I did find him. He has a hideout up near Canada, though *he* calls it a hunting lodge. He swore at me for ten minutes once I managed to raise him by radio.

Said he'd retired and was about to dust off that boardroom chair just as soon as he got used to being a married man. I said he'd never get used to it, and wasn't it nice? Anyway, I told him we were mobilizing the commando crew again and asked him if he wanted to play."

"Well, does he?" Josh asked.

"He's on his way. Shannon too. Do we have a plan, or will we charge blindly?"

"Charging Kadeira blindly," Josh pointed out, "would probably *not* be the best way to do it."

"Agreed." Kelsey joined them in contemplating the map, which had a course marked out from Key West to Kadeira. "So Hagen transported her by sea, huh?"

Raven indicated the marked course. "This is the only thing to approach Kadeira in the last forty-eight hours—just a boat. Anybody want to bet Sara isn't already there?"

After a moment Kelsey said soberly, "Are we sure she's there against her will? Absolutely positive? Granted Hagen's ruthless enough to kidnap her, but would Sereno have done it this way?"

Josh looked at him intently. "You tell us."

Kelsey glanced from Josh to Raven, then sighed. "He's a cagey one, Sereno. Awfully hard to get a firm handle on. Where his country is concerned, I sure as hell wouldn't want to get in his way."

"But," Raven said, "you spent more time around him than any of the rest of us."

Slowly Kelsey replied, "Where Sereno is concerned, Sara Marsh is the wild card in his deck. I just don't know."

"From instinct," Raven urged. "What do you *think*?"

"Well, I think that in the past he's gone to the extreme of making certain she was never forced in any way. Now . . . Dammit, it just doesn't feel right! This sudden move after two years. It's out of character. Unless . . ."

"Unless what?" Josh asked.

Behind mild eyes, Kelsey's mind was working swiftly. "Unless," he said softly, "she was in danger here. If Sereno believed she might be in danger here, he'd move heaven and earth to get her under his wing where she'd be safe."

They looked at one another in silence.

Sara requested a dinner tray in her suite rather than face Andres again that evening, and though Maria was clearly unhappy with the request, she nonetheless brought the tray upstairs without comment.

It was hardly something Sara could continue for the duration; four weeks was a long time to hide out in a few rooms. In any case, her own personality would not have allowed such an action. But tonight . . . tonight she couldn't face him again. She felt raw. For two years she had managed to convince herself that leaving him was the best thing she had ever done, and now she wasn't sure of anything at all.

She didn't allow herself to think about it at first. She ate dinner, then set the tray outside her door. She listened to some of her tapes while absently pacing the room. She caught herself listening for a knock at the door and was so unsettled by this realization that she turned the music up louder and swore beneath her breath.

The evening dragged on. She took a leisurely bath, filling the suite with the scent of jasmine, and felt like crying when she discovered jasmine sachets in the drawer where her sleepwear had been kept. With a peculiar sense of defiance she put on a long silk nightgown and sheer negligee in emerald green, ignoring the fact that it was Andres's favorite color on her.

Or had been.

She couldn't avoid thinking any longer about the Andres she remembered so well: a handsome, charismatic man with a low laugh and a glow in his dark eyes that she'd never seen in the eyes of any other man. A man who had requested that she wear green often because she looked "so damned beautiful" in the color. A man who had ordered dozens of rosebushes because she loved them, and never mind the difficulties of growing roses in a tropical climate; the roses had been kept alive and well for two years. A man who, when caught by the international press nakedly wearing his supposedly cynical and ruthless heart on his sleeve, had reacted with rueful amusement.

He had told her he loved her less than an hour after their first meeting. He had proposed marriage an hour after that. And yet it had been nearly a week before he kissed her, a week filled with media attention that had unsettled her. Andres had been unfailingly courteous to the reporters, but blandly uncommunicative; she merely had been disturbed.

At the time she had seen his invitation to come with him to Kadeira as an offer of escape from the media, and because he fascinated and charmed her, she had accepted. Yet even then she had sensed something dark inside Andres, something that both attracted and repelled her. Common sense had told her that a man who had won his country's leadership with his own hands had to be touched by a certain ruthlessness, yet she had not allowed that knowledge to prevent her from becoming involved with him. He intrigued her.

And here on Kadeira she had seen glimpses of that darkness, though never in relation to herself. He was, she had discovered, passionately devoted to his country, and quite definitely ruthless in seeing to its good. The revolution still attempting to depose him had had its beginnings more than a year before they'd met, and Sara had seen him deal with some of the problems it caused.

The rebels had infiltrated the one weekly newspaper of Kadeira; Andres had immediately shut it down and allowed only international newspapers, shipped in weekly, to be available to his people. The television station, picking up and broadcasting international programs by means of a satellite dish, had been captured and used for propaganda three times by the rebels before Andres, lacking the manpower to protect it around the clock, reluctantly closed it. The radio station was taken off the air for the same reason. He strictly curtailed trade with other countries because the danger to their ships was great, and he adopted a policy of politely but firmly warning off casual visitors to Kadeira.

The majority of the people of Kadeira, loyal to Andres, went about their daily lives as best they could. Unlike many other dictators, Andres taxed his people as little as possible, using every other means at his disposal to raise the necessary money to keep his country going.

Including . . .

The house was quiet, and it was long after midnight. Sara opened the French doors of her little balcony and stood out in the warm night, listening to the silence.

Finally facing herself, she silently agreed with at least one thing Andres had said in the gazebo. He was right in believing that she wanted the answers to be simple ones. Yes or no; black or white; right or wrong. But what she wanted was impossible in the real world. He said truth wasn't simple, and she knew he was right about that.

If life was simple, Andres, who undeniably loved his country, would have looked at the havoc of revolution and quietly stepped down just to stop the destruction. But it *wasn't* simple, and he couldn't do that. Lucio had made it obvious that his own regime would be a merciless one. So Andres remained in power, struggling daily and sometimes ruthlessly just to keep his people fed, clothed —and alive.

Right or wrong?

Sara leaned on the balcony railing and sighed as she looked down onto the darkened terrace. Then she saw a glowing red ember and realized that Andres was there, smoking one of his thin cigars and watching her. Before she could draw back into her room, he spoke.

"Shall we play the balcony scene from *Romeo and Juliet*?" His quiet voice reached her clearly in the silence, not really amused, not really teasing.

After a moment she said steadily, "Let's not."

The red ember flared brightly as he drew on the cigar, and his face was revealed in a faint but hellish glow; in that instant he looked so implacably dangerous that she caught her breath.

"No. I suppose not. It doesn't really suit us, does it?" He gave a low laugh, half sitting on the balustrade behind him to look up at her; he was almost directly below her, and only a few feet separated them. "For us, it's *Much Ado About Nothing*."

Sara swallowed, but the ache in her throat remained. "Which line?"

"A line for you? That's easy. 'I see, lady, the gentleman is not in your books.' " Andres laughed again, mockingly this time, and flicked his cigar out into the garden. "My line is easy as well." He drew an audible breath and his voice lost its mockery, rasping over the simple words. " 'I do love nothing in the world so well as you; is not that strange?' "

Sara straightened and took a step back toward the doorway, conscious of her heart pounding and her eyes stinging. Damn him! How could he make her feel this way when—

"Sara." He spoke quickly, still a little rough. "Walk with me in the garden?"

"No." She fought to steady her voice. "I'm not dressed, Andres. I—"

"It's dark. No lights, no moon. Come down, Sara, please."

She wasn't sure, even after she withdrew into her room and closed the French doors, if she would go out to him. She wasn't even sure when she found sandals in the closet and put them on, or when she left her room and went out into the softly lit hallway. It wasn't a conscious decision. And as she walked through the library to the open terrace doors, she knew why she had refused any and all contact with Andres after leaving Kadeira.

Because she had known that if he had once said "Come to me," she would have gone, in spite of everything. Just the way she was going now. And she knew why. Yes or no; black or white; right or wrong—truth wasn't simple. Not simple, and never to be avoided even if it hurt.

His verses from Shakespeare triggered something in her mind, something she had read here in this room and had not forgotten because the words had rung so utterly true. Lines written by Elizabeth Barrett Browning.

And a voice said in mastery while I strove . . .
"Guess now who holds thee?"—"Death," I
*   said, but there*
The silver answer rang . . . "Not Death, but
*   Love."*

The silver answer . . . And love, like death, couldn't be avoided or denied. Ever. She could no more resist going to him when he called to her than she could resist the next beat of her heart. And nothing could change that stark, simple, painful truth. Whatever he was, whatever he had done or would do in the future, she loved him.

When she had left Kadeira and him, her numbing anguish had come less from the knowledge of what he had done than from the knowledge that she loved him—*despite what he had done.*

"Sara?"

Standing on the terrace, she watched him walk slowly toward her, and her mind screamed in silence, *I can't let him find out!* She was afraid. That darkness in him, that implacable ruthlessness, would cause him to use the knowledge of her love against her, and she couldn't let that happen. She couldn't live with him as he wanted, marry him. She couldn't be with him through the years, loving in this kind of pain. It wouldn't destroy her love, but it would, in the end, destroy her.

She wasn't strong enough to love him.

"What is it, Sara?" His voice was low, and his hand grasped hers gently as he reached her side. "What's wrong?"

"Nothing, Andres." She heard her voice, light and mocking, and prayed that her control held. "Nothing at all."

After a moment he led her down into the garden, walking slowly along the path that wound in a relaxed pattern through three acres of fenced and patrolled grounds. "Have you become so brittle because of me?" he asked abruptly.

"Brittle?" Very conscious of the warmth and strength of his hand, she tried to concentrate on something else. But it was difficult; someone's hand was trembling, and she was very much afraid it was hers. "I'm two years older, and a hell of a lot wiser. What did you expect?"

Andres carried her hand to the crook of his arm and tucked it there, and she was a little relieved because at least now he wouldn't be as likely to feel her shaking through the linen of his white shirt. Oddly enough, it occurred to her only then that she shouldn't be touching him at all, that it wasn't safe. But she didn't retrieve her hand.

"Sara, in spite of everything, I don't think we want to tear at one another for the weeks we have together. Do we?"

"No." She sighed. "No, I don't think we do. Sorry, I seem to be the one doing all the tearing." In a voice containing all the calm she could muster, she added, "We made a bargain. It's over between us."

Andres didn't respond for a few moments, merely walking slowly beside her. When he finally spoke, it was in a contemplative tone, faintly wry but deliberate. "I suppose I should follow the rules this time. Play the game. Agree with you—or allow you to think I do."

"What are you talking about? It *is* over—"

"No, it isn't. We both know that, Sara. It didn't end when you ran away, it just stopped."

"We made a deal!"

"Yes. That you would remain here willingly for a month. I'll keep my part of that bargain. In a month, if you wish to leave, I won't try to stop you. And if you leave, I won't interfere in your life again. That was my bargain, Sara. I've never, at any point, agreed that it was over between us."

Sara halted, jerked her hand away, and turned to face him. Her eyes had grown accustomed to the darkness, and she could see him fairly well. He had also turned to face her, his head a little bent, and the shine of his dark eyes was like the surface of bottomless twin lakes, mysterious and potentially dangerous.

As evenly as she could manage, Sara said, "I'm leaving Kadeira in four weeks, Andres."

"Unless I convince you to stay."

"You can't. You won't."

He reached out suddenly and caught her in his arms, pulling her hard against him. "Can't I?"

Sara caught her breath and then lost it, dizzyingly aware of strong muscles and the hard heat of his body pressed to her own. In the first shocked moment she couldn't draw away, couldn't even try. Two years ago Andres had not taken advantage of the strong physical attraction between them, had not used desire to sway her. Not then. But this time, she realized hollowly, this time he would.

"No! Andres—"

"You've given me no choice, Sara," he said huskily. "I'm fighting for my *life*. And a soldier uses every weapon he can find."

"*Weapon*," she repeated bitterly, pushing against his powerful chest in an attempt she knew to be useless. "Is that how you see it, Andres? Sex is just another weapon to bend someone to your own will, to get what you want?"

"You've made it a fight," he told her, his voice growing ragged, strained. "I didn't want it this way, but if it has to be, I know how to fight."

"You won't win, not this time!" Sara didn't try to wrench herself free, because she knew only too well that his strength would defeat her, but she kept her arms stiff and fought to hold on to the anger.

"Won't I? Look at what you're wearing, Sara."

She went still, catching her breath and forcing her voice to remain steady. "I told you I wasn't dressed. I didn't expect to see you, to come out here—"

"You could have changed," he said softly but insistently. "But you didn't, did you, Sara?" One hand remained at the small of her back, holding her easily in place, while the other slipped between them and toyed with the thin ribbon tie of her negligee. "A woman wouldn't wear this to walk with a man she hated, would she? Not something like this, meant to be worn in a bedroom. And not his favorite color. It is green, Sara; I saw that while you stood on the balcony. My favorite color on you."

She could feel his touch between her breasts, toying with the ribbon until the negligee fell open, and she could feel her arms weakening, the strength of them slipping away. She couldn't move, couldn't even breathe, and the warm night was suddenly hot, closing in on her. "No." Her voice emerged in a whisper. "I just wasn't thinking. I—"

He traced the vee neckline of her gown slowly with his knuckles, the soft caress trailing fire, and the hand at her waist held her lower body tightly against the hardness of his. She was melting in the heat, the heat of the night and of him. Melting, and she couldn't seem to stop it. She tried to think, tried to remember why this was wrong, why she couldn't let it go on, but her thoughts were fogged, sluggish.

"You never let me see you in something like this before," he murmured. His hand brushed the full curve of her breast, separated from his flesh only by thin, sheer silk. "Why not then, Sara? And why now?"

She didn't have an answer, at least not one she

was willing to give him. "Don't. Andres, please." The last remaining strength in her arms gave out, and like a warlock, he knew the instant she could not longer resist him.

Even as both arms surrounded her, drawing her completely against him, his head bent and his mouth found hers. Before, Andres always had kept a tight rein on his desire, offering her only gentleness; now it seemed there was little gentleness left in him. His mouth was hot, hard, demanding. He kissed her with all the untamed force of his desire, and it was like a jarring blow that left Sara reeling.

She lost something then but didn't know what it was. Then she felt it leaving her, torn away by his implacable demand. And even though an answering fire in her matched his demand, even though her senses were vividly alive, her emotions were numbed by the sheer, overwhelming power of his desire.

It was like a sudden storm that blew up out of nowhere, battering her until she couldn't even fight to save herself, until she was left bruised and bewildered.

"You think you know the worst of me, don't you, Sara?" he muttered against her throat. His big body shuddered once, and he held her tightly. "But you don't. And you don't know the best of me."

Dimly Sara realized that her arms had somehow wound around his waist, and the knowledge that she was holding him with what strength she could muster was a distant shock. She had to stop this, had to—

"I could take you now." He lifted his head, staring down at her with eyes that burned even in the night. "I could, Sara. You wouldn't stop me. You wouldn't even try. And with this between us, you couldn't bring yourself to hate me in the morning. You know that, don't you?"

She stared up at him, hearing the voice that had moved a country. Hearing the voice that moved her and tugged at everything she was. "Yes," she whispered finally. "Yes, I know."

Three

The admission, made with bitter reluctance, quivered in the air between them. She forced her arms to release him, let them drop limply to her sides. Even now, with full knowledge and understanding of the consequences, she couldn't stop him. And it wasn't only her body that demanded his with an aching insistence; her heart, too, longed for a consummation that, if not complete, would at least leave her with something when all this was over and she was alone again.

Andres's hands rose slowly and framed her face. His eyes still burned, but his voice was suddenly gentle and deep, and his hands trembled against her flesh. "I know. Heart of my heart, I know. But *you* must know the best of me now, my love. I could never, would never, hurt you that way. I could never take from you anything you were reluctant to give me."

"You said it yourself." Her voice was soft, still,

lost somewhere. "I couldn't stop you, wouldn't even try. And I wouldn't hate you for it."

"No," he agreed, touching her lips with his in a fleeting tender kiss. "You wouldn't hate me. But something between us would be damaged beyond repair. Trust, perhaps. My love, I couldn't bear it if you gave me only a part of yourself."

Sara swallowed hard, a dim and instinctive terror stirring inside her. "You want everything, don't you, Andres?" That darkness, that blackness in him swallowing her . . .

He made an odd, rough sound. "Don't. Don't fear that, my love. Don't fear me."

She wondered vaguely if she had stiffened physically, or if he had become even more adept at reading her face, her thoughts. And it was, finally, the bewildered fear inside her that found a voice for itself. "You want too much," she whispered. "You ask for everything from me, yet you— No. I can't." She felt cold inside, and frightened, and she struck out because there was no other way to fight him. "I won't give my soul to the devil when he hasn't one of his own!"

Andres flinched as though she had slapped him. He stepped back, his hands falling from her face, and turned away from her in a jerky motion.

"*I'm sorry!*" The words were torn from her in horror; she felt sickened by her own cruelty. "That was . . . unforgivable."

"Do you really think me a devil?" he asked, low.

"No. No, of course not." Sara had her arms folded protectively against the sudden chill of the night. She was conscious of the hot trickle of tears down her cheeks, and it felt as though some vital barrier inside her had ruptured. "Please . . .

please, Andres, stop this. Stop me. Let me go."
She wasn't even sure what she was saying, except
that it had nothing to do with leaving the island,
but she was at least sure of the knowledge that
they could hurt each other so terribly.

"I can't." His voice was strangely calm.

"You have to." Her recognition of the awful power
they held over each other made her voice shake.
"Don't you understand? I'm like an animal in a
cage trying to tear my way out. I—I'll hurt you
without meaning to."

"Sara . . ."

"I can't give you what you want! There's too
much between us, too much I don't understand,
too much I'm afraid of." She dimly wondered where
her anger had gone. Now there was only this sense
of desperation, this terrifying recognition that they
were both somehow connected—and caught up in
something that neither could control. "I don't have
the strength for this!"

Andres slowly turned back to face her, though
he didn't step closer. In the dimness of the garden
he was a shadowy presence, big, curiously fea-
tureless. "You have the strength," he said in a
deep, still voice. "You *must* have it. I can't stop
this. I can't let you go. You haven't realized . . .
Heart of my heart, the love I have for you is the
best of me. And what will I be if I lose that?"

Sara couldn't breathe, couldn't move. His words
shocked her, frightened her, moved her unbearably. The understanding that she was so terribly
important to him was a burden, and she stag-
gered under the weight of it. "No." Her voice almost wasn't there. "No, don't say that."

"I have to. You must know it."

She realized she was backing away from him only when she felt the jab of a bush behind her, and when she put her hand back automatically, the pain of caused by thorns was barely noticeable. He had forced from her the admission that she wanted him too badly to be able to fight him, or even to hate him afterward; she had shown him her own vulnerability where he was concerned, had given him the power to hurt her dreadfully.

But Andres had stripped away his armor as well, with a single, jarring admission of his own, and with that admission he had given her the power to all but destroy him.

"Sara . . ."

She was running, and she didn't stop until her bedroom door was closed behind her. But she didn't escape him. She couldn't run away from him this time, she knew. This time there had to be an ending between them.

Late the following morning, Captain Siran, who had remained in his small boat that had been tied up at the dock overnight, sat on the cramped bridge writing a short note. He was ready to leave Kadeira and head back toward Key West, and manners required that he inform his host of his intentions. Manners, and the fact that Sereno's naval fleet took a dim view of boats leaving the harbor without proper permission.

Siran would have used his ship's radio to inform the president, but Sereno had sent word that his enemy could intercept radio transmissions now because of recently acquired equipment, and that it perhaps would be wiser to tell Lucio as little as possible. Captain Siran had no problem with that—except for one small thing.

That morning Hagen had radioed a very brief message.

Out of habitual caution the federal maestro had coded his message, but Siran was still bothered by the possibility of interception. Chances were good, of course, that Lucio wouldn't have understood the message even if he managed to decóde it. But if he *did* understand . . .

Hagen, Siran reflected, had made a bad mistake this time. The situation could be defused if he'd only tell certain people things in order to placate them—but Hagen was notoriously unable to be open and aboveboard about *anything*.

Siran didn't like any of it. But there was nothing he could do about the situation, and he had his orders. So, along with his intentions of leaving, he added a brief message to Sereno: "From Hagen via radio this morning: Please be advised Long and company very distressed over disappearance of Miss Marsh. Their intentions unclear at this point. Past actions demonstrate they may take the matter into their own hands. Yacht *Corsair* projected to be in your area."

Siran went out on deck and beckoned to a nearby lieutenant. "Can one of your men take this note to President Sereno?"

The burly man nodded agreement. "Teo has been our messenger since the president forbade radio contact; I have a message to send as well. Leaving, Captain?"

"On the tide."

"Good fortune."

Siran nodded. "Thanks. And to you." He watched

the soldier stride toward a group of men near the warehouses, continued to watch as a younger soldier climbed into a battered jeep and drove away. Then, sighing a little, Siran turned back to his preparation to cast off.

Thinking of the lieutenant's good wishes, he muttered, "May fortune favor the foolish." But nobody heard him.

Colonel Durant was frowning a bit as he handed the slip of paper back to his president. "Long? I didn't realize he knew Sara. It was the other one he knew, the woman who looked so like her."

Andres shook his head. "I shall have to ask Sara, but I believe Long and his friends became interested in Sara's well-being after Rafferty and his wife visited here. Of course they'd be concerned when she vanished, particularly if they know or suspect that she was brought here against her will."

"Nevertheless," Durant said, "what could they hope to do? Impossible to reach the island without our knowing—"

"They did once before," Andres murmured.

The colonel was silenced but only briefly. "Under cover of a storm. And Long himself didn't risk coming to the island."

"The Final Legion was here then. It isn't now."

Durant's frown deepened. "But the revolution exists; he would be in danger, and men of his wealth are cautious."

Sereno smiled just a little. "Vincente, in an hour or so Joshua Long could raise his own army—by comparison to which both mine and Lucio's would be pathetic."

"He wouldn't. International law—"

"International law aside, no, he wouldn't. But he could, if he chose. And a man such as he could, I imagine, find his way to Kadeira in caution and relative safety."

Accepting that, Durant asked, "We expect him, then?"

"We won't be surprised if he arrives."

Durant studied his old friend in silence for a moment. This new threat to the island was worrisome enough; Vincente was concerned over Sereno himself. The president seemed very tired, drained emotionally rather than physically. He had said nothing when Sara had failed to appear at breakfast, but his eyes had strayed often to the place that had been set for her.

The colonel had seen Sara slipping out into the garden a few minutes ago, and she had looked as drained and haunted as Andres did. Clearly there had been a confrontation of some kind between them, and just as clearly, it had resolved nothing. And Vincente was worried because if they both showed such strain after less than twenty-four hours . . .

"I need to ask Sara about Long and his friends." Andres's voice was slow, almost reluctant.

Durant understood the hesitation, and it didn't surprise him only because he, more than any other, knew just how strong Andres's feelings for Sara were. So he understood now that Andres was diffident about approaching Sara alone, even with so innocuous a reason, after whatever confrontation had so shaken the both of them. But perhaps, Durant thought, it was just what they needed—an impersonal topic to discuss.

"Shall I find her for you?" he asked.

Sereno was concentrating on a munitions inventory before him on the desk, and didn't look up when he answered in a low voice, "Thank you, Vincente."

Sara had slipped into the garden because she was getting claustrophobic in her suite. She had paced the floor all night, unable to sleep or even to rest. And now she wandered in the garden, touching a shrub here, a flower there. Trying not to think but thinking all the same.

During the long hours since she had run from him the night before, Sara had come to at least one certain realization: Whether or not she somehow came to accept Andres's actions two years ago in allowing the terrorist group a sanctuary here, there was still the part of him she was afraid of, the darkness. And she couldn't live with a man she feared.

"The love I have for you . . . is the best of me."

If that was true . . . she could destroy him. Or at least destroy that part of him she loved, that charming, intense, gentle part of him. Just as she had done the previous night, she would, in her own panic, tear at him in her efforts to fight this between them, to escape him. She'd say cruel things, strike out at him. "I'll not give my soul to the devil . . ." She would batter his love until it lay around them both in ruins.

". . . what will I be if I lose that?"

If she killed it, then . . . then she'd see the worst of him.

Sara wondered, dimly and tiredly, if that was

what really drove her. Did she strike out at him, tear at the gentle layers of his love, because her fear compelled her to know the worst of him before she could love without reservation?

He hadn't shown that side of himself to her, whether consciously or not. But it was *there.* She sensed it, had glimpsed the darkness from time to time in fleeting moments. She knew it was there.

She tried to remind herself that some of the most monstrous leaders the world had known had loved passionately and even tenderly in their lives. That didn't change them, didn't alter what they were. So it shouldn't matter to her that Andres loved her, that he was gentle with her.

But it *did* matter.

She had to see him clearly, had to understand everything he was. She couldn't trust her instincts, because those instincts were in chaos. And she couldn't run away again. There had to be an end to it, one way or another. This time it couldn't just stop.

Yes or no; black or white; right or wrong. She had to see, to know and understand, the worst of him. There weren't any simple answers, weren't any easy solutions. And they could hurt each other so dreadfully.

"Pardon, Miss Marsh?"

Sara jumped in surprise, the heavily accented voice causing her to swing around. He was a young soldier with a shy smile and curiously flat back eyes, bobbing in an awkward bow.

She forced her muscles to relax. "Yes?"

"The president, Miss. He asks that you come."

She nodded, preceding him along the path he

indicated. And it wasn't until they'd nearly reached the corner of the house that Sara wondered abruptly why Andres would have summoned her to the area where the cars were kept parked—the only area at the front of the house that the perimeter guards couldn't see.

"Wait a minute. What—"

She discovered quickly enough the unexpected strength of the young soldier. And the quickness with which he clapped a sickly-sweet cloth over her nose and mouth defeated her before she even could begin to struggle. After that was only blackness.

By the time he had searched the entire garden, Colonel Durant was worried. It was unlikely that something had happened to Sara, but Durant preferred to err on the side of caution. And she had slipped away from these very grounds once before.

He went back into the house, asked a quick question of Maria, and, despite the negative answer, went up the stairs two at a time and rapped sharply on Sara's door. There was no answer. He went in, quickly searching the suite. Empty.

He returned downstairs and hurried to Andres's office where there was an intercom connected to the guardhouse at the gate. When he burst into the room, Andres looked up in surprise.

"Vincente? What—" He broke off, his face going tight and pale. "Sara."

Durant leaned over the desk to stab the intercom button. "Morales."

"Colonel?" the gate guard responded instantly.

"Has anyone left the grounds in the past hour?"

"Only Teo, sir."

Durant's eyes met Andres's, and both held the same realization—Teo, the trusted messenger, his uniform giving him safe passage, would have gone unquestioned through the grounds.

"Did you search his vehicle?"

"When he came in, sir." Morales sounded puzzled, apprehensive.

"Not when he left?"

"No, sir." Definitely apprehensive now. "But, sir, he was driving a jeep with no top; we could see inside."

"You're absolutely positive he was alone?"

"I—there was a tarp in back, sir. But we checked under it when he came in. There was just some equipment, some sleeping bags." After an instant's hesitation Morales added stiffly, "We did wonder why he didn't take the harbor road—"

Andres spoke harshly. "Gather half a dozen of your best men, Morales, and get up here."

"Yes, sir!"

Woodenly Durant said, "He could have discarded the equipment out near the cars; no one would see it. If he knocked her out, hid her under the tarp . . ."

Andres reached for the radio behind the desk with some thought of contacting his patrols in the city but hesitated and looked at Durant. "He has no means of contacting Lucio, but if I order the men to find and stop that Jeep, Lucio will know something has happened, and he'll guess it has to do with Sara."

Durant nodded. "You don't dare risk it."

There was a big automatic in a webbed holster in the bottom drawer of Andres's desk; he got it out and stood, buckling the belt in place. And his voice, when he spoke again, was a bleak rasp. "She may have gone willingly, Vincente. She may have run away from me again."

Durant couldn't deny the possibility. "She must be found."

"Yes. Yes, she must be found." Andres's mouth twisted bitterly. "So that I may *protect* her."

Every breath Andres drew burned in his chest and caught raggedly in his throat. Every passing second was an eternity filled with anguished terror. She was gone, taken from him. She was gone, and he could barely think, could hardly feel past the numbing cold of his fear for her. He was vaguely aware that Durant protested when he got into an open jeep but ignored his old friend's worry over enemy snipers.

The jeep all but stood on two wheels as it shot through the open gate and turned hard onto the harbor road, then shuddered with the strain when it was almost immediately turned again at right angles onto the rougher road Morales had indicated that led to the beach before swinging back inland. It was a little-traveled, treacherous road, marked by hard-baked hillocks thrown up by the mud slides of the rainy season and by eroded gullies that were invisible until a vehicle was quite literally on top of them and unable to stop.

From the moment Morales had indicated Teo's choice of route, Andres had been conscious of desperate urgency, and he pushed the old jeep to its straining limits. They could, if they were quick enough, catch up to Teo before he even knew he was being followed. But if he saw them and increased his own speed in an effort to escape . . . He was an inexperienced driver, and his chances of avoiding all the dangers of the road at high speeds were virtually nil.

But if they didn't catch him, if he reached the jungle's edge ahead of them, then he was gone. After years of war Andres knew only too well how easily an army could be hidden in those impenetrable depths; a lone vehicle would seem to disappear completely.

The stress Andres was placing on his jeep made the engine roar like a tortured thing. Only the seat belt he had automatically fastened kept Andres in place as they hit the worst of the road and the jeep defied the laws of gravity in its bouncing, jarring attempts to become airborne.

He heard Durant cursing steadily beside him, heard the grunts and muffled exclamations of the machine gunner behind him who was holding on grimly to his gun. But Andres was oblivious to everything but urgency and fear.

And then they topped a rise, and in the instant before the jeep plunged downward into a hollow, he saw Teo. The young soldier was no more than fifty yards ahead of them and going at a reckless clip, his jeep bouncing and slewing wildly.

"Andres, for God's sake!"

He barely heard Durant, concentrating on squeezing the last possible ounce of speed from his laboring engine. With an iron will and sheer determination he held the jeep on the road when it should have gone off, and at a speed that was nothing short of suicidal. After a sharp incline the road ended temporarily to become the beach, turning back inland nearly a mile farther down the coast. Andres never slowed. The last bend before they plummeted down onto the beach nearly finished them, the engine screaming shrilly when all four wheels left the ground. Then they were on the beach, level and smooth, and Teo was no more than twenty yards ahead of them.

Andres's feeling of triumph was short-lived.

Ahead of Teo's jeep, far down the beach where the road began again, was a small band of heavily armed soldiers. Lucio's soldiers. Whether or not they recognized Teo and knew he was bringing them a prize was unclear, but they instantly fanned out, dropped for cover in the rocks by the road, and opened fire.

Andres's machine gunner, well trained, immediately brought his own gun to bear on the soldiers, and the staccato chatter of his gun rose above the laboring scream of the jeep's engine. Andres barked out a harsh command to stop the gunner, sickly aware that the angle was deadly, that the soldiers in the rocks weren't high enough above them to make shooting past Teo's speeding jeep a safe exercise.

The angle was indeed deadly. The soldiers, aiming toward Andres's jeep and the one behind, couldn't possibly keep Teo out of the line of fire. And it was inevitable that at least some of those men, few of whom were expertly trained or skilled marksmen, would hit the closer jeep.

Teo's vehicle slewed furiously until it pointed toward the sea, rose up on two wheels, and shuddered violently. Then it flipped over with a grinding crash and rolled over several times, finally coming to rest in gouged-out sand, its wheels spinning futilely in the air.

Andres felt something tear loose inside him, some sound, some part of himself. The jeep slid jerkily as he locked the brakes, not even aware that Morales and his men had sped past, guns firing at the band of soldiers hurriedly withdrawing from the beach. He was aware of nothing, not time or motion or events.

He would be told later that his seat belt had been wrenched cleanly from its floorboard bolts, that he had left the jeep and approached the wreck with such inhuman speed that his men afterward swore that his feet never had touched the sand. And he could never explain later, even to himself, what guided him away from the wreck when he had seen nothing thrown from it. But something guided him, or called to him, because he found Sara yards from the overturned jeep.

She was a limp, tarp-wrapped bundle hidden behind a jagged rock that rose from the sand. She didn't move when he dropped to the sand and muttered her name, or when he worked with awkward haste to untie the ropes that kept the tarp around her.

She didn't move when he threw open the tarp, when a hoarse cry broke from him like something dark and dreadful on the wind.

Her head hurt terribly, and her whole body felt sore and bruised. She thought she smelled jasmine but decided it was a dream. The voice was a dream, too, a dream slightly out of focus, because that wasn't his voice. His was a deep and commanding voice, sometimes gentle, sometimes hard, but it was never like this, broken and afraid and holding such pain. Never like this. So it wasn't his, of course.

She listened, idly, to the voice. The words it was saying were halting, as if half forgotten or long denied, Spanish words with an old, old cadence despite the erratic pauses. Her head hurt so much that she didn't try to translate with her uncertain Spanish, yet the meaning of the words seeped into her mind without volition and with surprising clarity. Praying. The voice was praying, and it wasn't accustomed to praying at all.

Floating, hurting, she nonetheless felt powerfully moved to look at the face the voice belonged to, because it was curiously familiar—yet unfamiliar. She tried to open her eyes, failing at first. But then there was a lightening of the darkness, and the scent of jasmine grew stronger. With an enormous driving effort she forced her eyes to open.

Her room. Her room in Andres's house, and that was why the jasmine. Her bed beneath her, blessedly soft against bruised flesh. And how had she bruised herself? Her head hurt.

The voice was more distinct, and she forced her aching head to turn, with agonizing slowness, until she could see him. There was something wrong with what she saw, and she was fretful because she felt she should understand why it was wrong. He was . . . he was kneeling. By her bed. He was holding her hand in both of his, his head bent over her, shoulders bowed, his familiar voice broken and hurting in an unfamiliar way, saying old words in a half-forgotten prayer.

And it was wrong because . . . because a devil with no soul couldn't shed tears, even in an awkward, unpracticed way.

She felt a new pain, somewhere deeper inside her, and tried to tell him not to do that, not to hurt her like that. But her voice wouldn't come. Then he looked up, his ashen face tracked by tears, his black eyes so anguished that she would have cried out against such suffering if she could have.

For an eternal moment their eyes locked, and Sara felt a sudden easing of something, a curious sense of acceptance. Something that had bothered her terribly slipped away, even as she felt her eyes closing, even as she mustered her last strength to respond to his gentle grasp by tightening her fingers slightly. And she thought to herself as she heard his voice fade away that words of love in Spanish were wonderful to take into dreams.

Her lovely dreams were disturbed at some point by voices, one of them steady and competent, the other rough and urgent. Something painful was done to her head, and she cried out half consciously. The rough voice, softened and hushed now, soothed her gently until the pain eased.

"Aftereffects of the chloroform. Shock. Bruises. Eight stitches in the head wound. And scalp wounds always bleed a great deal. A concussion, certainly."

"Will she be all right?"

"Wake her up at least once every hour, just to be sure. If you can't get her to respond, call me immediately."

"Dammit! Will she be all right?"

Sara lost the conversation at that point, drifting away from it disinterestedly. She was vaguely aware of time passing. His voice called her now and then, and she always managed to rouse herself enough to murmur his name, though her eyes refused to open again for a long time.

A soft knock at the door half woke her some undetermined time later, voices reaching her clearly despite the lowered tones.

"Teo was killed, shot. Impossible to tell if it was our guns or theirs. We've recovered his body, Andres. Do you wish—"

"Send him back to his family." Andres's voice was flat and hard. "Not in uniform. Not even a dead traitor may go home wearing the uniform he betrayed." There was a slight pause, and then Andres added in the same tone, "Make certain everyone knows, Vincente."

"Very well, Andres."

Sara drifted away again, troubled by what she had heard.

It was night when she saw the room again, the lamps turned low and everything silent. And Andres was standing by the French doors leading out onto the balcony. Awakened by the throbbing of her head, she lay and watched him, as still and silent as he was himself. Someone had dressed her in the green gown, and she decided not to ask who had done that. She thought she knew, anyway. She watched him.

He looked so tired, she thought, so drawn. He had pulled back the filmy curtains with one hand and seemed to be looking out through the doors, but his gaze was blind.

She remembered, then, two strangely vivid

scenes, one seen and heard, the second only heard. In the first, Andres as he had been beside her bed; in the second, his flat, hard order that had sent a dead soldier home stripped of his uniform and all honor.

"Andres?"

He turned instantly, crossing to her bed, his eyes anxious but his expression masked by control. "Sara, how do you feel?" His voice, too, was controlled.

She watched as he sat carefully on the edge of her bed. "I feel sore. And tired. What happened?"

"One of—of my soldiers seems to have been in Lucio's pay." Andres's voice was low. "He took you out in the back of a jeep, hidden in a tarp. We followed. During the chase some of Lucio's soldiers opened fire down on the beach. Teo was shot, the jeep overturned. You were thrown out. You had been injured, struck on the head either during the wreck or earlier—"

"It must have been during the wreck." She wasn't surprised that in Andres's voice and in his mind there could be the faintest question, the inescapable idea that she might well have had a hand in her own apparent kidnapping. "He told me you wanted me at the house, and it wasn't until we'd nearly reached the cars that I wondered why you would have called me there. That's when he—chloroform, I suppose."

"Yes. Some was found in the wreckage of the jeep."

He had accepted her explanation instantly, she realized, and with a relief strong enough to penetrate through his control and show briefly on his lean face. She thought of that young soldier. "You sent . . . Teo . . . back to his family. Without his uniform."

"You heard that." It wasn't a question. His eyes shuttered themselves. "Yes, I did. He was a traitor, Sara."

The harshness of that disturbed her, but not as strongly as she had expected it to. She just wanted to make it *fit*, make it somehow a part of her unfocused image of him. "And if . . . if it had been my idea? If I'd asked Teo to get me out of here? Would he still be a traitor?"

"Yes," Andres said flatly. "A traitor to *me*, Sara."

She thought about that, wishing absently that her head would stop pounding. Was Andres's action a harsh one under the circumstances? The leader of a revolution-torn country had to be certain of his army, yes; and treachery couldn't be condoned or forgiven. In Andres's world his action made sense.

"Sara, I'm sorry. I believed I could protect you here."

She looked at him, at the masklike face and shuttered eyes. His voice, she thought, gave him away, and she wondered if, with her, it always would. It was a curiously comforting thought. "You couldn't have known," she said finally.

He shifted a little, not quite a shrug, not quite a denial. "Perhaps. Sara, if you ever—if it ever comes to a point that you feel desperate to get away from me, tell me, please. If Lucio were ever to get his hands on you, I—"

"I won't run away again." Her voice was steady, certain. "I promise you that, Andres."

Doubt flickered behind the shutters. "No?"

She felt a smile curve her lips. "No. It doesn't seem to—to accomplish much, does it? As you said, nothing ended when I ran away before. It just stopped for a while. I've realized that I can't live like that. Neither of us can live like that."

He looked at her for a moment, and she thought he was undecided, although his face revealed nothing. Then, slowly, he said, "Have you made up your mind about us, then?"

Again his voice gave him away, and she didn't need to see braced shoulders to know he was half prepared for an answer that would be a blow.

She tried to find words, in her own uncertainty, to tell him what she felt. "Can you make up your mind about a hurricane? No. It just . . . exists. Either you run, or else board up all the windows and ride it out."

He smiled a little, not with amusement but with understanding. "Have you boarded up the windows?"

"I can't run this time." Clinging to the emotional safety of analogy, she said slowly, "And I don't know what will be left standing when it's over. Maybe I'll find out that I'm not tough enough to ride out the storm. But I have to find out. We both have to find out."

"Can I make it easier for you?" he asked quietly.

"Yes." She drew one arm from beneath the covers and put out her hand to him, feeling the warmth of his long fingers closing instantly around hers. A little unsteadily she said, "Don't muffle the thunder, Andres. Don't cloak the lightning. I can't hide from any of it—even if you want me to."

Four

Andres looked down at the hand he held and, after a long moment, softly quoted, " 'God be thanked, the meanest of his creatures boasts two soul-sides, one to face the world with, one to show a woman when he loves her.' Is that what you mean?"

How odd, she thought vaguely, that he should quote Robert Browning about love when she had earlier quoted to herself Elizabeth Barrett Browning about the "mastery" of love. And how strangely moving it was to hear this proud, self-educated man turn often to the wise words of poets to express his own deep feelings.

She drew a deep breath. "Yes."

His mouth twisted a little, and he didn't look up at her. "Should a man not show the softer side of himself to the woman he loves?"

Her fingers tightened in his. "Andres, it isn't

what I see that frightens me. It's what I don't see, what you won't *let* me see."

"So." He met her gaze finally. "You wish to see the face that took a country in bloodshed. The face that gave sanctuary to terrorists. The face that sent a dead boy home to his family branded a traitor for all to see."

She didn't flinch from his hard voice. "It's your face. It's you. Should either of us hide from that?"

"You wanted to," he reminded her almost reluctantly, his tone unchanged. "You tried. You ran from it in fear. We both know that. Do you really believe I'll allow the same thing to drive you away again?"

"Just because I can't see it doesn't mean it isn't there, Andres!"

"That part of me will never touch you." His voice was still harsh. "It doesn't exist between us."

Sara knew that Andres understood what she was afraid of; she also knew that his method of dealing with it would never be a solution for her. He couldn't—or wouldn't—defend his actions, perhaps because there *was* no defense, but he had seen her fear and had acted to banish it, taking care that the darkness she feared in him was hidden from her as much as possible. He could speak of it to her and would, but he would consciously try not to show it. Even now he was trying to shield her.

So she braced herself inwardly and said the only thing she could to show him how impossible his solution was. "You say you want my love, my trust; how can you expect that from me? How can I love what I don't understand? Or are you willing for less? Do you want me to love only a part of you, Andres?"

She hadn't flinched from his harsh voice, but he flinched from her quiet one.

Sara went on as steadily as she could. "I can't, you know that. Not and live with you." She suddenly wanted to cry. "I'd always be afraid of that part of you, always wonder about—about the darkness in you."

"Sara—"

"It's *there*. We both know it! You said I had to see the best of you; I have to see the worst too. I thought it was the terrorists, but you said yourself I hadn't known the worst of you. I have to."

"No."

"Yes." She steadied her voice with an effort. "Andres, I said I wouldn't run away again, and I meant that. But if you won't let me understand you—completely—then I'll never get over the uncertainty. I'd always wonder. And I'd have to say good-bye—this time—and *walk* away."

He said nothing, just continued to gaze down at the hand he held.

Sara searched his face and was conscious of a growing desperation. He'd shut her out, blocking the chinks so that nothing escaped, and she couldn't let him do that, not now. Not when it was so terribly important. "You said that I wanted the easy answers, the simple solutions," she said. "And you were right. I ran because there *weren't* any easy answers. Now I know there can't be, not between us. But there *has* to be understanding, Andres. And truth. You said that, too, that you'd have no lies between us."

"I've dug my own grave, haven't I?"

She felt a prickle of foreboding, an odd unease. His voice had been strange, almost lifeless, as if the metaphorical grave he spoke of yawned before him. But before she could speak, he was going on in the same tone.

"And if you can't live with the worst?"

She didn't say anything, because they both knew the answer.

After a moment Andres lifted her hand quickly to his lips and then released it, rising to his feet. His expression was hard-held, masklike, remote. "We'll discuss this tomorrow," he said. His voice was even now, controlled. "You should eat. Maria's kept something hot for you; I'll go and tell her you're awake."

Sara waited until he was at the door, then said, "Andres?" And when he half turned back to her, she said, "Tomorrow things won't be different."

His expression changed then, and for a flashing instant she thought of defeat, of something beaten. Then he was expressionless again. "I know."

She looked at the door for a long time after he left.

A considerable distance away from the tensions of Kadeira, a massive and dangerous-looking man moved with inherent grace through the shadowed streets of a large East Coast American city. No casual stroller of those streets would have seen him, but the petite, red-haired woman standing patiently under a streetlight spoke to him even before he left the concealing shadows and joined her.

"Well, did you meet your mysterious contact?"

"I met him." Unexpectedly, Zach Steele's deep voice was rather soft. "Anybody bother you, honey, or did that misbegotten hound pretend he was a guard dog?"

The "misbegotten hound," who was an Irish wolfhound, and who, at a hundred and fifty pounds, far outweighed his mistress, woofed softly in response to this aspersion on his character and thumped his tail lazily on the pavement. The redhead patted him consolingly and addressed her husband.

"Three men passed, and all of them scraped their elbows on that wall to walk around us. Wizard smiled at them. With all his teeth. Zach, did you get answers?"

He took her hand and they began moving down the quiet, shadowed sidewalk, Wizard pacing at their heels. "Interesting answers," he affirmed, his deep voice still soft. Then, as if continuing an old argument, he said, "You should have stayed in New York, Teddy. This trip has been so rushed, you haven't gotten any rest at all."

"I'll rest on the jet going back." And then, apparently addressing Wizard, Teddy Steele said dolefully, "One of these days he's going to find out that I was never meant to be wrapped in cotton or put under glass." Wizard woofed in doubtful agreement.

"Dammit, Teddy." Zach's voice roughened a bit. "It's only been a couple of months since . . ."

Teddy's voice softened. "I'm fine, Zach. Really. Now, what did you find out?"

After a moment, and after a reassuring squeeze of her hand, Zach explained what he'd found out.

"It looks like Hagen's goons snatched Sara about two jumps ahead of someone else. Two men, Latinos; they stuck out a bit in this neighborhood, so they were noticed."

"Sereno's men?" Teddy asked, then replied to that herself. "No, that doesn't make sense, not if he'd asked Hagen to bring Sara to him; he wouldn't have sent his own men after her as well. So who were they?"

"Hard to say for sure," Zach told her broodingly. "But I'll bet that if we backtracked, we'd find that Sara's been running from two different . . . parties—all this time. Sereno's men, certainly. And somebody else's."

Teddy, who was extremely intelligent and very quick at reading between the lines, exclaimed softly. "An enemy of Sereno's, maybe? Practically the whole world knows how he feels about her, knows she's his . . . one weakness. Could it be someone who wanted to get his hands on Sara to—to use her against Sereno in some way?" She remembered when it had happened to them, when an evil madman had used her as bait in an attempt to destroy Zach.

Zach's hand tightened around her as he, too, remembered. After a moment he said, "Could be. Kelsey said it didn't fit otherwise that Sereno would move all of a sudden after nearly two years—and that makes sense. If he found out somehow that his enemy was closing in on Sara . . ."

They walked in silence for a little while, and then Teddy spoke soberly. "You're worried Josh is going to go down there."

"I know he will. Hell, we're all suckers for love."

The words were flippant, even sardonic, but his tone wasn't. "And those two should have a chance; it'll be hard enough for them without some bastard trying to use Sara to break Sereno. They should have a chance. Josh'll go down there—Derek, too, I'd bet. Josh owes Sereno, and if this is all because he's trying to protect Sara, then I'm sure Josh wants to help."

Quietly Teddy said, "You can't wrap him in cotton, either."

"Yeah, I know."

But knowing it wouldn't stop him from trying, Teddy knew. She had known that from the first, had known that Zach would instantly and without thought or hesitation place his own large body between danger and anyone he loved. So she mentally began to gather her arguments, because Zach wasn't going to Kadeira without her; he just *wasn't*.

"Teddy . . ."

"The *Corsair*," she said serenely, "is very comfortable, after all. And I love islands."

"Dammit, honey . . ."

Sara was up and about the next day despite Andres's objections, sporting a white bandage just above her left temple but feeling much better physically. Emotionally she was still a bit raw, accepting what she felt, but still confused, still afraid that in the end she wouldn't be able to understand and love what she thought was the ruthless core of Andres, the part that gave him much of his enormous strength.

As for him, he avoided the "discussion" he'd

said would take place that day. Obviously he was still tired and drawn, and his eyes, when they rested on her, were watchful, wary, and yet somehow anguished as well, hurting. Sara was disturbed and worried, but she didn't press him, knowing that they needed time. There was so much between them, so much tension, so many feelings, so much pain. They were, she thought, afraid of that pain, both of them. Afraid of hurting each other even more. They were careful.

They were still being careful when Andres came looking for her sometime after dinner that night, finding her in the library, where she was trying to find a kind of peace among the poets. He sat down across from her in a chair and, asking her permission with a lifted brow, lit one of his thin cigars. She wondered only then where he had acquired his curiously old-fashioned manners, but she didn't ask.

She didn't ask because she was suddenly and rather bewilderedly coping with a stinging surge of feelings and sensations. The physical awareness between them had always been powerful, but since she'd returned, the strong emotions had partially masked—or even overwhelmed—desire. But it seemed now that the aborted kidnapping, or its disturbing aftermath, had changed that.

In the eternal instant during which he concentrated absently on lighting the cigar, she found herself looking at him as if she'd never seen him before. He was graceful even in his stillness, handsome in his weariness. The physical strength of him was a tangible thing, a vital force cloaked in fleeting quiet.

And in his eyes, those dark, intense eyes, were emotions that compelled, intrigued. Behind the shutters, underneath the wariness and the caution, the pain and the love, was the stillness of a man who had lived too long with danger. He looked at her then, and in the unguarded moment when their gazes locked, she thought she glimpsed his soul. It shook her to her own.

Love, instant and intense. Pride. Pain. And there was something else. Held in an iron grip, with the kind of desperation only a wounded soul could know, were the last tatters of illusion, the final, fragile tendrils of a cherished dream.

She tore her gaze away with an inner gasp, staring blindly down at her book. Too late, too late! It was always too late. . . . Embedded in her heart, as close as her own soul. If she hadn't come back, she still would have loved him all the days of her life, angry and afraid. But she was here, and the anger was gone, the fear turned to confused uncertainty.

"I wanted to talk to you about something, Sara," he said rather abruptly. "About Joshua Long and his friends."

She was a little surprised and welcomed the distraction. Laying her book aside, she said, "There isn't much I can tell you about them." Her voice was steady.

"You've met?"

"Face-to-face, only once," she answered readily. "It was a little over a year ago, months after I left Kadeira. . . ." She hesitated then, frowning a little.

Dryly Andres said, "I'll make it easier for you. You were contacted by an American agent—either by a man named Hagen or by Sarah Cavell herself. Sarah was to take part in a very covert assignment here; she was part of a team sent to rescue another American agent I was holding as a political prisoner. It was believed that her similarity to you would make it easier for her and Rafferty Lewis to get in and out of Kadeira safely. And successfully."

Sara was staring at him, a little puzzled, a little tense. "You— Did you know that . . . then?"

Andres hesitated, then nodded. "I knew. As soon as I saw her, I knew what Hagen had intended."

"You turned your back and let them escape, even though you could have stopped them," Sara said very slowly, remembering what Sarah Cavell had told her, gently, over the phone a few days after that escape.

He hesitated again. "Her resemblance to you made it easy for me," he said finally, tension evident in his voice. "No one was surprised that I couldn't allow her to be harmed."

Sara was trying to make sense of it. "But if you knew Hagen, knew why they were coming here— and Vincente said something about you having called in a favor from an American agent in order to get me here—then Hagen was returning the favor you did him, wasn't he? The favor of helping him to get his agent out of here safely. You *planned* that." She shook her head, adding softly, "Sarah said you did, that you were helping them, even though it wasn't supposed to look that way."

"It was for my benefit as well," Andres said, apparently unsurprised by that other Sarah's perception. His voice was suddenly flat. "Kadeira's benefit."

He's showing me, Sara realized, something in-side her tightening. *Showing me a little of the darkness.* She found that her eyes were fixed al-most painfully on his face, her ears straining to catch the shading of every word. And there was something else, something she sensed in him. This was important, so important.

"The last thing I needed," Andres said, his voice still hard, "was the United States as an active enemy. The terrorists wanted Kelsey; they would have killed him. Not to put too fine a point on it, but the U.S. wouldn't have liked that. It was all to the good, as far as I was concerned, to get Kelsey out of here as soon as possible. Without, I need hardly say, angering the Final Legion any more than necessary."

The last statement was, she thought, uttered with deliberation; Andres still wasn't prepared to "apologize" for having allowed the terrorist group a base on Kadeira. She nodded slowly but made no comment.

Abruptly the darkness was gone; having allowed her to hear motives that he had flatly maintained were largely selfish and self-serving ones, Andres veered to another subject.

"At any rate, you were going to tell me what contact you've had with Long and his friends." His voice was quiet and calm again, his face less masklike, curiously relieved-looking.

"It wasn't much. I talked to Sarah, of course, before they came here. And a few days after. It was—oh, I guess it was a couple of months later when they found me." She smiled suddenly, rue-fully. "Your people and, for that matter, Lucio's, could take lessons from Josh Long on how to find people who don't want to be found. I was feeling pretty safe at that point and was staying in a small hotel on the West Coast. I never even sensed I was being watched, but I must have been, because Sarah Cavell—Sarah Lewis by then—just appeared at my door one day."

"And?" Andres prompted when she fell silent.

"She was very kind." Sara cleared her throat. "She said they were concerned about me. That Josh and Raven Long, and their security expert Zach Steele, wanted to talk to me. She took me to another hotel, a big one, and that's when I met the others. Rafferty was there too. They offered to help me. Josh said it was possible to build a new identity for me so nobody would ever be able to find me, if that was what I wanted."

After a moment Andres said, "You would have been safe." His mouth twisted suddenly. "I thought I could keep you safe here, and within twenty-four hours you were taken from me. You should have accepted Long's offer, Sara."

She felt an abrupt surge of anger. "I should have? And just become someone else, like changing clothing? It was *my* life, Andres! *My* name. I might have run, but I always knew who I was. And I won't let anybody take that away from me!"

Her outburst seemed to have shaken him; his eyes were shuttered again, his face expressionless. And his voice was quiet when he said, "Of course not. And I'm sure they knew that, understood that."

Sara snatched at calmness, held on to it. Careful, she had to be careful. But she felt unsettled, and from more than the burst of anger. "They knew. Especially Raven, I think. Raven is Josh's wife. I thanked them but told them I didn't want that. They weren't surprised. They asked me to keep in touch, let them know how I was from time to time. And for a while I was in touch with Sarah. But not recently. Not since somebody—I don't even know who it was now, your men or Lucio's or Hagen's—almost caught me. I just ran after that."

"I see."

She looked at him, feeling puzzled again. "Why did you ask? Is it important?"

"Perhaps. I was alerted yesterday that Long and his friends are troubled over your disappearance and may take it upon themselves to act."

"Come here, you mean?" Sara frowned. "It doesn't seem likely. They hardly know me, Andres."

He smiled a little, the mask easing because they were being careful again. "I met Long years ago, talked to him. And I talked to him just before Rafferty and Sarah arrived. He is the kind of man who will always intercede when wrong things happen. As far as any of them know, you're being kept here totally against your will, possibly behind bars. He would care about that, I think, and wish to help you."

Sara dropped her gaze to the hands folded in her lap. But they knew something Andres didn't know, couldn't be sure of, she thought, something that might make them hesitate in any attempt to "rescue" her. They all knew she loved Andres, she was sure of that. Softly, without looking up, she asked, "What will you do if they come here?"

"If they come openly," he said in an even tone, "my ships will warn them off, just as they would any casual visitors."

"Warn them off—forcefully?" She looked up then, seeing his face change as they once again approached that darkness.

But the darkness didn't quite arrive, because Andres shook his head with a faint smile, with that same odd relief. "That wouldn't be wise of me, would it? I can only warn politely where men such as Joshua Long are concerned. If he chooses to ignore my warning, there is little I can do about it. I could protest to his government, I suppose, but even they tend to tread warily around such men."

After a moment Sara said, "If I could talk to them—"

"I don't dare attempt radio communication. Lucio is able to intercept the transmissions, and above all else, he must not know that one of the richest men in the world may be en route here."

"Damn," she said softly. Then, realizing, she said, "You really respect Josh Long, don't you? Not just what he is—but the man he is."

Andres nodded. "He wields great power, Sara— far more than most people realize. And he does it with grace. He has strength and commands absolute loyalty, but never through fear. His word is known throughout the world to be his bond—no exceptions. And he is, above all, an honest man." Andres's smile was crooked. "Not one man in a million possesses that unique melding of positive traits. I wish . . ."

"What do you wish?" she asked.

In a light, faintly self-mocking tone he replied, "I wish he could teach me just one of those traits."

"Which one?" she asked, knowing the answer.

"To wield power gracefully." Abruptly he got to his feet, and his voice had gone flat when he added, "You're right to fear the darkness in me, Sara. Power is a dangerous thing." He left the room before she could respond.

After a moment she picked up her book and opened it, gazing down on the pages blindly. Something, she realized, had happened. Something had changed.

"It was for my benefit as well."

"Power is a dangerous thing."

Careful; they had been careful. And yet . . . She had the odd feeling now that Andres had decided something the night before, had made up his mind, and was acting on that private decision. He had shown her a glimpse of the darkness in him, had spoken flatly of self-serving motives without apology. He had told her she was right to be afraid. He had never once spoken of love, had not used endearments.

"He's pushing me away." She heard her blank voice speaking aloud, startling her. But that was it, of course; that was what he had decided.

He was convinced she could never love the dark part of him, had been convinced all along, or else why hide it? Even now he was convinced. That was why there had been no endearments, no words of love. He was, with deliberation, with stony determination, pushing her away. And he was tearing himself up inside to do it.

Sara didn't doubt that Andres loved her. She

wondered, now, if she had ever doubted it. Probably not. She hadn't wanted to face it, hadn't wanted to accept it, but she had never doubted it. Andres loved her.

And he was trying to make it easier for her to leave him. Sometime during or after their strained discussion the previous night, he had simply decided that she would be better off without him, had perhaps come to the conclusion that she would leave, anyway, whether she came to understand him or not. And he had doubtless realized that neither of them would be able to cope with a slow, agonizing interlude before she finally left him. And this time the leaving would be final. There hadn't been an ending between them before; Andres was going to end it this time. He would end it with absolute finality, driving her away from him so completely that no shadow of love would remain to haunt her.

That was what he thought would happen.

The question was: Was he right?

Could she love the worst of him, whatever that might prove to be? She had run before, in fear. In fear that she could love a man who could do so monstrous a thing as house terrorists and take blood money from them. The voice in her mind was clear and firm, and she listened to it in dawning realization.

She knew the worst of him.

And the rest? Her wariness, her uneasy awareness of the dark strength in him, the ruthlessness? Was she truly afraid of these qualities, or was she simply afraid she loved even that about the man? No. it was something else. And she thought she knew, now, what she was afraid of.

She accepted, fully and for the first time, that she loved Andres. She had awakened to find him kneeling by her bed, had seen, just minutes ago, what might have been his soul. Nothing would ever be the same again. Her driven need to tear at him was gone, and she couldn't sit silently by and watch him tear at himself, convinced he was destroying whatever she felt for him, certain he was helping to end things for her with a minimum of pain.

Sara laid her book aside with unnatural care and got up from the couch. She left the library and went down the hall to Andres's study, knocking briefly before opening the door and going in. And she totally ignored the startled presence of Colonel Durant when she asked a stark question.

"Do you know that I love you?"

Durant melted away without a word, and Andres stood at his desk where they'd been working, studying a map of the island. He was looking at her, his face a hard mask and his eyes blank. He didn't go to her as he would have the day before, didn't move to touch her.

"Do you know that?" she asked again.

"Sara—" His voice was harsh with strain, giving him away as it always would.

"Do you know that I didn't run away from this island because you let terrorists stay here?" Every word emerged clear and calm, and she walked toward him slowly. "I ran because I loved you *despite* that, and it scared the hell out of me. It didn't seem possible that I could love a man who could shelter the very terrorists who had killed my parents and so many other innocent people. But I did, and I knew it. So I ran. It was too much, too strong, and it still is."

She stopped an arm's length away, looking up into the handsome face that was losing its mask, into eyes with no shutters hiding them. "I don't know if I can handle something that strong," she went on steadily. "I don't know if *I'm* strong enough. But I do know one thing. I can't let you tear yourself apart thinking that something inside you could destroy my love. I love you, Andres. And nothing could change that."

Sara wasn't surprised that he still didn't touch her, didn't move toward her. She could feel the tension in him, the battle to hold himself away from her. She knew why. Because the feelings were so violent. Because there weren't, couldn't be, any half measures between them; there were only complicated questions with complex answers.

"You're still afraid," he said finally, roughly. "Why do you come to me when you're still afraid? Is it pity, Sara?"

She knew he was remembering the night before and the broken, uncertain prayers by her bed. Knew he was wondering if that memory had brought her here. "You're too strong to be pitied," she told him quietly, honestly. "And, yes, I'm still afraid. The difference is that now I know why. Not of anything in you but of how I might react to it. I've never felt so strongly before, Andres. How you make me feel is so frightening—the power of it, our ability to hurt each other. It's a—a kind of bond, and there's no escaping it."

"Is that what you want? To escape it?"

Sara shook her head a little. "I tried before, Andres, and I couldn't. Even if you hadn't brought me back here, I wouldn't have escaped it. I would have kept running, but I wouldn't have gotten away from it. From you."

"But is it what you *want*?" he asked harshly, demanding an answer to that torturous question. "To escape?"

"No, not anymore." Her voice was very soft. "I've realized I love you too much to want that now. But I have to know that I can give you everything you need without losing myself. Don't you see? I have to match you, balance you, or I'll be overwhelmed by you. You're stronger than you know, Andres. And much of that strength comes from the intensity in you, the ability to be ruthless when you have to. I have to face it, find out if I can understand and cope with it, or it's no good— it'll never be any good. If I'm not strong enough to love you, we'd be better off apart. *That's* what I'm afraid of."

She took a deep breath and lifted her chin. "And that's why I won't let you push me away, Andres. I won't let you hurt yourself, or me, by trying to end it. You can't end it."

His hands rose, as though they had minds of their own, and rested very carefully on her shoulders. "You said you had to see the worst of me," he reminded her, his voice still rough.

Sara hesitated, shaking her head a little and thinking of the clumsy uselessness of words when feelings were so powerful. "I do. But, Andres, I'll never see anything in you to make me hate you, or be afraid of you. I know that. I think I always knew it. I just have to find out if I'm strong enough. Do you remember in the garden when I said I didn't have the strength for this? You said I had to have it, and you told me—"

"That the love I have for you is the best of me?" he said, finishing for her.

She nodded jerkily. "Yes. To feel so much takes strength, Andres. It isn't a tame thing between us, a gentle thing. Nothing in my life prepared me for you."

"Sara!" his hands tightened on her shoulders, and she could feel a tremor in them. "My love, you have strength, great strength. I know it. I feel it."

She half closed her eyes in relief at the endearment, knowing only then that he wouldn't go on trying to push her away. Until that moment she hadn't been sure she would win. "I have to be certain," she whispered. "I have to know that I'm strong enough to handle this, strong enough to give you everything you need. Just give me a little time?"

Andres pulled her into his arms and held her very gently. "As much as you need," he murmured huskily. "Even if I have to steal it."

Sara knew what he meant. Time was a luxury in Kadeira; Lucio and his army made every single day's survival a victory. She also knew that this new and fragile understanding between them had to be protected and nourished if it were to survive, and that they were both raw and vulnerable right now from everything they had fought their way through. They both needed time. Even if they had to steal it.

She drew away slowly after a moment, smiled at him before moving around the desk, putting needed space between them. And her voice emerged more naturally than she would have believed possible when she spoke. "You and Vincente were working on something when I interrupted. Why don't you get him back in here, and I'll just sit and listen."

Andres was watching her, smiling, his face more tranquil than she had yet seen it. And his black eyes were burning, intense, hungry. Softly he said, "I can barely think when you're in the same room."

Sara caught her breath, felt the leaping response of her heart. But she was light, careful. "You'd better learn to," she murmured, and wandered over to the shelves of books he kept near his desk. She heard a quiet laugh from him, then his footsteps as he left the room. She chose a book at random and went to sit in an overstuffed chair.

How easily he makes love with words! Like no other man she had ever met, he held her captive. Intrigued. Enthralled. Was it Donne who had said something about never being free until—? She frowned a little, then looked at the title of her book and laughed aloud. She wasn't surprised to find Donne among the pages, and to find the quotation she had half remembered. "Take me to you, imprison me, for I, except you enthrall me, never shall be free. . . ."

She slowly turned the pages of the well-thumbed book, wondering how many times Andres had searched here and found, as she did, the words of kindred spirits struggling with similar baffling emotions. They shared a love of words, but Andres had the better command of them. Probably he could talk the devil out of hell, she thought, given a few moment's grace and a fan to hold back the flames.

She looked up as Andres and Colonel Durant

came back into the room, faintly amused to see the colonel eyeing her a bit warily. "I won't blow up in your face, Vincente," she told him gravely.

Andres chuckled as he moved to his desk, and Durant followed his president, murmuring, "No. You already did, I think."

Sara smiled and bent her head over the book again, reading a line here, a verse there. And she listened as Andres and his colonel went back to work, quickly realizing they were trying to pinpoint Lucio's most recent camp from their knowledge of previous ones and of the terrain. It was a slow, frustrating business, hampered by the sheer size of Kadeira's jungles and by Lucio's almost magical ability to hide within them.

She only half listened at first. Gradually she felt more and more of herself drawn toward the desk. And Andres. She felt his gaze on her from time to time, as tangible as touch. She heard, as always, his voice give him away at such moments with tiny breaks, almost infinitesimal lapses in the rhythm of his sentences to Vincente. And she could feel, as if her own mind had wandered, his struggle to gather strayed thoughts into coherency.

"I can barely think with you in the same room."

It was desire. She knew that because she felt the effects of it herself. But it was also more. It was an affinity, a *connection* between them. The unnerving awareness of being a part of another mind and heart, less alone than before, and so vulnerable because of it.

No wonder she had run. Cut Andres and she would bleed; hurt him and she would feel the pain. And she knew it was the same for him, knew it from an anguished voice in her memory saying broken prayers at her bedside.

And from other voices, other memories.

" 'I do love nothing in the world so well as you: is not that strange?' " His voice had been rough with feeling.

Yes, strange. How very strange, she thought. They hadn't been looking for it, either of them. In truth they hadn't wanted it. But it had them, captured, compelled.

She hoped she was strong enough for this, hoped it desperately. Because, just like Andres, if she lost this, she would lose the best part of all she could ever be.

Five

When it became obvious that Andres and the colonel were going to be up very late working over their maps, Sara quietly excused herself, deciding to go to bed. Andres came out into the hall with her, closing the office door behind them.

"You should rest," she told him, anxious.

He was leaning back against the door, looking down at her. "Lucio is a threat to you, Sara. I have to remove that threat."

She was tired and knew she should go to bed, but she lingered, wanting to look at him, talk to him. "When you do defeat him, what effect will it have on the revolution?"

"It will be over."

Sara was surprised. "Is he so strong a leader?"

Andres shook his head. "Only partly. He *is* a strong leader, but the point is, he fights out of hate, Sara. There's no burning sense of injustice driving him, no all-consuming dream of a better world. It's said that in every revolution there's one man with a vision; Lucio isn't the man."

"Then why do his men follow him?"

"Sheer habit." Andres sighed tiredly. "They've known nothing else, most of them. Only fighting. And he's the flag they follow into the only life they know."

"Then, when he's gone?"

"He hasn't a single lieutenant strong enough to take over as leader. His army will scatter into the jungles and hills. After a time, when they learn that I mean to exact no vengeance, they'll come out of hiding."

"You won't punish them?" She wasn't surprised somehow.

"How could I?" He smiled faintly. "I followed a leader into revolution, became one myself."

"But you had a vision," she said in a soft tone.

"I thought so." After a moment Andres said quietly, "In any case, with Lucio gone, the fighting will end. For a while," he added with faint bitterness. "Until someone else comes along, full of hate. Or seduced by a vision."

"Does it have to be that way, Andres?" She was trying to understand. "On and on with no end—just moments of peace and hours of war?"

"Without change, yes. And change takes time, Sara. If I can keep the peace long enough, if I can show my people there *is* a better way . . . If. Always *if.*"

Sara instinctively reached out her hand to him, hearing first the passion of commitment and then a return of the faint bitterness of frustration in his remarkable voice. She reached out her hand and touched his lean cheek, feeling a muscle go tense beneath her touch, seeing his black eyes flare briefly before they were half hidden from her by lowered lashes.

"If anybody can pull this country together, you can," she told him. "Some thing are worth fighting for."

Andres didn't move to touch her, but his hooded gaze was a tangible caress. "This is," he said huskily.

Sara forced her hand to leave him, nodding half consciously. "I know. Good night, Andres."

"Good night, my love."

He stood still, watching her move down the hall toward the stairs. When he could no longer see her, he turned, finally, and returned to his office and his colonel.

In the penthouse office of a gleaming high rise in New York City, a group of people sat around and talked with the easy camaraderie of those who have been through much together and emerged with close ties. It was late; outside the floor-to-ceiling windows the lights of the city glittered, and inside the building the normal hum of brisk business was muted by night.

The conversation had been going on for some time, and it had, finally, more or less come down to who would go to Kadeira and how. It had come down to what they knew and what they could do. The "if" had been decided long before.

Josh Long turned away from the windows and rested a hip on the corner of his desk. "It's no use calling Rafferty and Sarah back from Australia even though we could use their help," he said to the others. "I'm guessing that by the time they could get back, it would be finished. Besides, they haven't been there long enough to get over the jet lag."

"We can't all go to Kadeira, anyway," Zach pointed out mildly. "That is, if any of us goes at all."

Josh looked at him, his flickering smile an indication of the understanding that Zach would prefer at least two certainly not to go, that Zach still thought there was an "if" in the matter. Then he looked at Kelsey, lounging in a comfortable chair and frowning at nothing. "Kelsey, are you sure that captain of Hagen's came clean with you?"

Kelsey stopped frowning at nothing and nodded. "Sure as can be. Siran wasn't happy about the situation at all, and he's—well, sort of an old friend. He told me all he knew. This enemy of Sereno's, this Lucio, has the ability to intercept radio transmissions. And Hagen sent a coded message to Sereno by way of the captain, warning that you just might be en route to Kadeira. Or words to that effect."

"Which means Lucio also might know," Zach said in a determinedly conversational tone, apparently to the room at large.

"If he broke the code," Josh added.

Derek Ross, the most recent arrival to the penthouse, along with his new wife, Shannon, said lazily, "Not a hard code if I know Hagen."

Josh looked at the big blond man sitting on one of the two long couches beside the delicate Shannon. "How hard is not hard?" he asked.

"That," Derek replied, "depends on Lucio. If he knows anything at all about codes, he'll find

Hagen's pretty much child's play, particularly if he speaks good English."

"He does," Kelsey said. "Quite good English."

"Damn," Zach said.

Josh was frowning. "Okay, look at it this way. Maybe Lucio could and did decode the message. So what?"

Zach swore again. "So you'd make a hell of a valuable hostage, that's so what."

"You have a one-track mind," Josh told him dryly. "Think, Zach. What the hell would Lucio want with me?"

From her comfortable and usual seat in Zach's lap, Teddy asked, "If he can get Sara, you mean?"

"Exactly." Josh gazed around the room at his friends. "From all we can find out, this so-called revolution is just a feud to Lucio. He wants Sereno deposed and destroyed—period. And yesterday wouldn't be fast enough to suit him. If he can get his hands on Sara, that'll do it. And you can bet he knows it. I'm not saying that under normal circumstances he wouldn't think of a lucrative kidnapping to help fill his war chest, but I'm willing to bet his mind is on Sara right now."

"Willing to bet your life?" Zach asked.

"What about *your* life?" Josh retorted.

"That's different."

"No. You just think it is."

Lucas Kendrick spoke quietly as he leaned on the back of a couch behind his wife, Kyle. "For what it's worth, I agree with Josh. There's a risk, but not much more than usual."

"Traitor," Zach muttered.

Luc grinned faintly. "Sorry, Zach. Look, we can minimize the risk; we always do that, no matter what."

"Place is a fortress," Kelsey commented almost idly.

"Sure," Lucas agreed. "But we can't change that, not without declaring—and winning—an all-out war. So we've got two choices when it comes to getting into that fortress. We take the *Corsair* and hope Sereno's navy doesn't have orders to sink any approaching ships. Or we take the jet helicopter and drop right down in his lap."

"Antiaircraft guns," Zach said in objection.

"Why would he have them?" Lucas asked reasonably. "Lucio doesn't have a plane to his name; there isn't even a landing strip on the island. And God knows nobody else has bothered to attack Kadeira by sea *or* air."

"There's a relatively easy way to find out," Derek said. "General Ramsey thinks the sun rises and sets on this crowd after the mess down in Pinnacle was cleared up so fast. Call in the favor. He can have a reconnaissance plane do a flyover of Kadeira and take some nice clear pictures. Infrared and the like. Within a few hours after he sanctions it, we'd know exactly what's on the island."

Josh smiled in approval and looked at Zach. "Well?"

"It's all right as far as it goes," the big security chief said. "But how about all the guns that'll be pointed our way once we get out of the bird? Lucio is one thing; what about Sereno? Think he's going to stand tamely by while we offer Sara a lift out of there?"

Kelsey, frowning at nothing again, said quietly, "I think he will. Not tamely, no; he isn't a tame man. But if she wants to leave, especially in Josh's charge, he'll let her."

Raven, who was sitting in her husband's chair behind the desk, said suddenly, "She loves him, you know."

Josh looked back at her. "Yes, that was my impression. Still."

"Still," she agreed, "she wasn't asked, she was taken. And Siran said she was mad as hell."

"It's the revolution," Shannon said suddenly. She looked up to find everyone gazing at her quizzically, and she flushed slightly. She was still new enough to this group to be a little shy among them, a little uncertain, but her own recent experiences made her feel deeply for Sara Marsh.

Derek smiled down at his wife. "What about it, honey?"

Drawing courage as always from those loving, wise old eyes, she smiled in return and looked back at the others. "It's at the center of everything," she said. "It cuts Kadeira off, isolates it. It's dangerous to Sara because she can be used to hurt President Sereno. He knows that. Think of the pressures on him, on them both. They can't—they aren't let alone to be just a man and woman. And they should be."

After a moment of silence Kyle said quietly, "There's that. We can offer Sara a choice. We can get her out of danger, at least for a while. And what have we solved? They'll be apart again, and she'll be on the run as long as Lucio—or someone else—wants to hurt Sereno. Shannon's right. It's the revolution."

Josh lighted a cigarette and, surprising no one, said tersely to Kelsey, "What'll it take to stop the revolution?"

"Lucio dead or otherwise taken out of action,"

Kelsey answered without hesitation. "That'd do it, at least for a while. Because, this time, it's a feud, as you said. Then—time and money. Given both, Sereno could get the economy on its feet, and his people would likely be satisfied once they saw progress being made. That island's good raw material for another Caribbean paradise. But, hell, Josh, after half a century of revolution, who's going to pour money into that island?"

"Someone," Derek said lazily, "always can."

Zach said very dryly, "No doubt someone will."

Ignoring that comment, Josh said, "Lucas, Kyle, you two handled General Ramsey last time. How about it?"

"The reconnaissance flight? Sure," Lucas said, and Kyle nodded.

"All right, then," Josh said. "First thing in the morning, here's what we'll do."

And he told them. Zach didn't like it, of course; he much rather would have gone to Kadeira alone. Without an ounce of conceit in his soul, he still preferred to slay dragons himself and keep friends and loved ones away from the beasts. The only problem was those friends and loved ones were dragon slayers too.

They wouldn't be put under glass.

Dammit.

Sara endured a slightly painful visit from the doctor the next morning, was pronounced recovered and fit. The bandage over her temple was replaced with a smaller one, and the doctor said the stitches could come out in a few days. Sara wasn't surprised by the doctor's verdict of recovery since she felt fine, but she was glad the report eased Andres's obvious concern.

She and Andres were still being careful of course. But the reasoning behind their caution was different from the previous day. Then, both had half hidden behind walls; today they were cautiously building a bridge.

Yet Sara was conscious as never before of the hunger in Andres's eyes, and very aware of the matching hunger in herself. Like everything between them, it was too strong to ignore, too complex to rest placidly under the convenient label of desire. It had filled her dreams during the night, an ache that wouldn't leave her. It hovered all around today, sharpened by abrupt stabs of longing.

Part of her wondered why they waited, but another part of her was still troubled by a lack of understanding. She felt strongly that the more she understood him, the more solid their bridge would become.

And there was so much about him she needed to understand. Not just the worst of him, but rather what brought the worst *out* of him. What drove him? What vision had sent a young man to war in determination? How had he become the man he was? And what was it that he would lose if he lost her?

Questions she could ask him, certainly. But she thought she should find the answers for herself— and she didn't know how to do that.

The morning passed. Aware that her nearness was a distraction, she left Andres and the colonel to their work that afternoon. She went out into the garden where the early coolness was burning away under the heat of the sun and found the old gardener, Carlos, at work among the roses. Happily, he remembered her and carefully explained in his halting English how he had grown her roses for her.

Sara borrowed gloves and tools, working along with him and listening to him as he talked to both her and the plants impartially and with affection. She was scarcely aware that the sun grew hotter, and she looked up with a start when a shadow fell over her.

Andres bent to place a wide-brimmed straw hat atop her head before she could say a word. "You've forgotten the sun again," he said, half scolding.

Carlos loosed a stream of rapid Spanish to his president, his tone contrite, and Andres responded briefly in the same language, kindness in his voice. Then he looked back down at Sara. "Carlos is aghast that he forgot you were unaccustomed to the sun," he told her.

"It wasn't his fault. I forgot too."

"That's what I told him."

Sara shook her head as she reached up to adjust the hat. "I really should learn Spanish," she said, half to herself.

"I'll teach you, *mi corazón.*"

She looked up at him questioningly.

"My heart," he translated, smiling.

Sara wondered when it had gotten hard to breathe; she hadn't noticed until now.

Andres didn't seem to expect a response. "Don't stay out here too long, Sara. Just because the doctor said you were recovered doesn't mean you shouldn't take care. All right?"

She nodded and watched him stride back toward the house. He must have seen her from the window of his office, she realized, and had left Durant waiting while he went to find her hat. Almost absently she leaned forward to continue weeding the rose bed, half hearing Carlos as he went on talking to the plants.

But even as she worked, Sara glanced up from time to time, seeing in the distance a glimpse of the high iron fence, hearing an occasional shout or laugh from one of the soldiers walking the perimeter. She saw that the parapet of the house was manned now, as it hadn't been when she'd arrived; half a dozen soldiers paced warily, alert.

This was Andres's life. With peace in his land, could he achieve tranquillity in himself? Perhaps. But Andres was a man of power, and men of power are always targets; Sara knew that. So there would always be guards and fences and caution. She had learned caution these last years, had learned to be wary—but she had been free. She had been able to walk public streets alone, had eaten in restaurants, had sat peacefully in theaters and parks. She had been a target only to a handful of men who saw her as a tool.

If she remained with Andres, everything would be different.

Was love strong enough to survive in a cage? Was *her* love strong enough? And was she, herself, strong enough to commit her life to loving a man of power, a complex, charismatic man who would always be a target?

It all came down to that question, as well as her lack of understanding. And Sara didn't know how to find that answer, either. Time would provide it, but time was a doubtful commodity on Kadeira. Yet what could she do? She had asked for time even though she knew how uncertain it was, even though she knew that they couldn't long remain in limbo.

But how could she discover the extent of her own strength? There was no mountain to climb here, no ocean to cross or battle to be won; there was no single, definitive test of her courage. She had the hollow feeling that if ever there would be a moment of blinding certainty when she could say, "I'm strong enough," it would occur far in the future, with years of life's testing behind her.

She couldn't wait for that. Andres, offering a total commitment of his own, would accept no less from her—and deserved no less.

"Why do you come to me when you're still afraid?"

Restless, Sara returned the gardening gloves and tools to Carlos and thanked him, then went back to the house. In the kitchen, Maria scolded her for staying out in the sun too long, gave her iced tea, and chattered brightly while Sara obediently finished the cold drink.

She felt, peculiarly, that a veil had been drawn between herself and everyone else, that she was looking through it at a world with softened, blurred outlines. Colors were muted, sounds muffled. It was as if the world were unreal, distant, pushed away by the conflict raging in her mind. And the struggle within her seemed to gather energy, force, swirling with a violence that pushed the world even farther away. She felt still, rooted, trapped in the tiny eye of a hurricane while she waited for the storm to overtake her.

Leaving Maria with polite thanks and hardly noticing the housekeeper's worried look, Sara wandered through the house. She passed the closed office door without glancing at it, fearing that the sheer force of her longing would somehow summon Andres to her. She was too bewildered to face him now.

She went up to her suite and took a cool shower, then changed into white shorts and a green terry-cloth tank top. Brushing her hair automatically before her dresser mirror, she noted idly that her outfit was revealing. As if it were someone else she saw, she studied golden flesh, slender curves. She looked at her face with detachment, wondering what was there to command the love of a man. It was a face, her own and familiar. Green eyes and a small nose, and a mouth that looked vulnerable.

She turned away from the mirror and, barefoot, padded out into the hall and then to Andres's room. She had never been inside this room but opened the door without hesitation and went in. She was vaguely conscious that she was looking for something, searching for answers she badly needed.

She felt Andres as soon as she stepped across the threshold. This was the private sanctuary of the man rather than the open office of the president. Here he slept, here he dressed, and, in the bathroom off to the left, here he showered and shaved.

Sara closed the door and wandered slowly around the room, settling finally in a big chair near the foot of the bed. Like most of the furniture in the house, this room contained old, massive pieces, gleaming softly with the patina of age and care. The bed was a huge four-poster, the chest as tall as she was, the dresser long. There was a shelf filled with books near the door, an eclectic collection ranging from poetry and the classics to works on the tactics and strategy of war.

But Sara wasn't looking at the furniture or books; she barely noticed the thick carpet or the drapes drawn back from the French doors leading onto the balcony. She looked instead at a single wall across from her chair where a large framed oil painting hung. It was easily viewed from this chair and from the bed, and she wondered how often he stared at it.

She had no idea where he could have gotten it, or who had painted it. She thought it had probably been privately commissioned by Andres years ago, perhaps just after he'd come to power. She knew only that she was gazing on the vision that had carried Andres through a revolution—and through all the years since.

The painting was of Kadeira, but it was not the Kadeira she had seen. It had been painted from the angle of the harbor, with the only real city on the island as the focus. And there were no shorn buildings, no bombed remains of cars or trucks, no rubble. And no scars showing through the whitewash. This was a city with gleaming windows and clean-swept streets, small shops open for business, and smiling people moving along the sidewalks.

There wasn't a soldier, a gun, or a jeep in sight. Nor, Sara realized, was this a painting of vaulting ambition; there were no signs of great wealth or well-heeled tourists. There was a small hotel on the right near a ribbon of beach, but it wasn't a glass-and-steel monster meant to house the rich;

it was tucked away in the lee of a hill, pretty and pleasant and no doubt comfortable. In the distance, between jungle and mountains, there was a tilled field here and there; in the foreground a fishing boat sailed toward the dock, riding low in the water with a satisfying catch. Children played on the sand.

Sara swallowed hard, feeling her throat ache. Andres didn't ask for much, it seemed. Unlike some leaders, he didn't seek to make his country a great power. He only wanted his people to be comfortable, well fed, safe, and happy.

She looked at the little hotel again, realizing suddenly that it almost existed, that it was one of the buildings she had seen that had been partly constructed before the rebels had gutted it.

He was trying, she thought. Trying so hard. And she felt an abrupt, grinding hatred for Lucio and those like him, hating them for coming between Andres and his beautiful dream.

The tatters of illusion in his eyes, his soul. The last fragile tendrils of a cherished dream.

She was barely aware of shadows lengthening in the room as the sun set outside, staring at the painting and hurting inside. It was worth fighting for, that dream.

". . . the love I have for you is the best of me. And what will I be if I lose that?"

Sara realized, slowly, that she finally understood Andres. And understood what she meant to him. His dream had sustained him for a long time, a goal to work toward, but discouragement and bitterness were growing. In his efforts to achieve his goal, Andres had clamped down harder and harder, taking ruthless steps out of necessity. One step forward for every two he was driven back. And that would harden a man, even a good man; that would bring out the darkness of his strength.

Under the enormous pressures and frustrations of his life, Andres had been changing, slowly becoming the ruthless dictator he had never wanted to be. His reputation had been at its worst just before they'd met; she knew that now, although she hadn't known then.

And she realized that Andres had recognized what was happening to him. Perhaps he had looked into a mirror, and a man out of his nightmares had looked back. How that would have shaken him, hurt him! And then, in the midst of his disillusionment and growing bitterness and despair, he had found her. Because of her he had found in himself the capacity to love completely, deeply. And that simple yet complex emotion had halted what might well have been the total erosion of all that was good in Andres.

He needed her in a way she was only now beginning to understand. He had been so terribly alone with his dream, so locked inside himself because of external pressures. He couldn't stop, couldn't turn and retrace his steps; from the moment Andres had had a vision, his goal had been set. He wasn't a man to be easily turned. But he had been alone, and he had seen a face in the mirror he had never wanted to claim as his own.

He didn't need a cheering section, didn't need a validation of his dream from her; what he needed was the love that proved to an anguished spirit that he could never be the monster he was afraid of becoming. That was why he had hidden so much of himself from her, why her awareness and fear of the darkness had hurt him so deeply—because she saw and recognized what he was afraid of himself.

He needed an understanding love, a love that would see him clearly and never falter in that understanding. A love that could share the shadows as well as the light, the fears and uncertainties as well as the strengths. He needed a partner, a mate, a lover, a friend.

And she? She needed him. She needed the bond between them, the strange, compelling affinity, the closeness. She needed his love, complex and demanding though it was. She needed to hear his voice, to see the intensity in his black eyes, to watch him move. She needed the only man who had ever enthralled her, intrigued her, angered and hurt her. She needed the passion and tenderness he offered. She needed his sharp intelligence, his soft laugh, his crooked, charming smile.

She needed, beyond all reason, the careful balance between them, that dangerous, potentially painful high-wire act that would demand the best of them both to succeed.

He didn't offer a tame love or a tame life. He offered struggle, danger, great joy, and possible anguish. He offered a life torn by war, with no promise that ending this battle would prevent the one waiting just around the next corner. He offered enemies that would be hers as well as his. He offered an uncertain future.

He offered his love, a love that had never faltered in all the time they had been apart. A love that had stood with granite certainty against her fear and panic. A love he would never abandon, because it was the best of him.

And for Sara, when the moment of certainty came, it was neither blinding nor what she had hoped for. But it was an answer of sorts, and one that couldn't be denied. She didn't know if she was strong enough to give Andres all that he needed, to love him without losing herself, but she knew one thing, knew it with everything inside her.

She wasn't strong enough to leave him again.

"Sara?"

The lamp by the bed came on, and Andres straightened, relief easing his features as he saw her curled up in the big chair.

She looked at him, remaining silent, feeling the hunger, the sharp stabs of longing. He moved like a cat, she thought, watching him come around the bed toward her, as if he still moved through the jungles he had practically grown up in.

"Sara, dinner will be ready—" He stopped suddenly, didn't move or speak, gazing down at her with an arrested expression.

She vaguely wondered what her own face looked like to bring such anxiety into his. "I shouldn't have come in here without asking," she said. "I'm sorry."

He shook his head. "You're welcome anywhere in this house, you know that. Sara, what's wrong?"

She rose from the chair slowly, unable to stop staring at him. "Wrong? Nothing. I didn't want to bother you while you and the colonel were working, so I came in here."

"Sara—"

"I love the painting."

After a moment he said, "I'm glad."

She drew a deep breath, then stepped forward suddenly and slipped her arms around his waist. Instantly his arms closed around her, and she hid her face against his neck and breathed in the clean, faintly musky scent of his skin.

"Sara?"

"I want to belong to you," she whispered.

His arms tightened almost convulsively, his voice abruptly harsh with strain. "Sara, if we become lovers, I'll never be able to let you go."

She lifted her head, looking up at him gravely. "Yes, you would. If I asked to go, you'd let me. But I won't ask, Andres. I won't ask."

He caught his breath. "Are you sure?"

"I'm sure." Her smile was slow. "I love you."

"*Mi corazón . . .*" His head bent, his lips finding hers in a kiss that was unutterably tender. His arms drew her closer, one hand sliding up her back and beneath the heavy weight of her silky hair, while the other hand slipped down to her hips.

Tenderness heated, exploded into driven passion. His mouth slanted across hers, his tongue possessing her with a shocking intimacy; his big body shuddered hard, shaken by a wave of need. Sara felt her own body shiver violently, felt the hunger inside her surge with the breathless force of a tidal wave. She wasn't close enough to him, couldn't get close enough; she was frantic with the need to become a part of him.

She could feel the physical power of him; feel the hard muscles of a lifetime's brutal, daily struggle for survival; and was dimly surprised that there was no fear in her of his vital force. Instead she was seduced by his unthinking power, moved unbearably by the certain knowledge that he reined that potent strength for her.

A soft, primitive sound tangled in the back of her throat when his lips finally left hers, and she forced herself to release him long enough to cope with the buttons of his shirt. He was exploring the soft flesh of her neck, and she threw her head back, eyes half closed, her trembling fingers unfastening buttons with blind knowledge. She felt rather than saw him shrug the shirt off, and his powerful bronze chest drew her hands like a magnet.

The strength of him . . . It had made her wary, had intrigued and compelled her, had once frightened her. Now his strength was a tactile delight, igniting her senses, bringing her entire body vividly alive. The corded power of his arms held her, muscles rippling beneath bronze flesh. The mat of black hair on his broad chest was sensuously abrasive, and—

Scars. More than twenty years of war and hardship had left their marks on his soldier's body. Some were old, some more recent, but all were marks of terrible suffering.

Sara felt a sob catch in her throat, and she half pushed him away, her hands exploring, her eyes seeing for the first time. She had never seen his bare torso. "You didn't tell me," she whispered, hurting with the pain of those old wounds. "Oh, Andres—"

"Shhhh." He held her face, kissed her gently. "Old hurts, my love. From long ago. They don't matter now."

They mattered to Sara, mattered because his

life had held such pain. Yet he hadn't lost his
dream, not completely, hadn't lost the ability to
love. Unaware of her tears, she pressed her lips
to a puckered bullet scar on his shoulder and
then the thin white line of an old knife wound
high on his rib cage. And there were others she
could feel, marks on his back that she knew, with
cold instinct, were the scars of long-ago beatings.
The revolutionary army he had been yanked into
as a teenager had been a brutal one, led by cruel
men.

Oh, God, the pain!

"Don't," he said huskily, shaken, drawing her
close and holding her for that moment with
tender comfort. "Don't weep for me, Sara."

She realized then that no one ever had wept for
Andres, and it almost broke her heart.

"Love me," she whispered, fierce, driven. Her
body molded itself to his, yielding, seeking. She
met his lips with burning need, barely tasting
the salt of her own tears. She wanted to give and
give, to overwhelm him with her love until even
the memory of pain was gone. She helped him
draw the tank top over her head, heard the rasping sound he made when she pressed her naked
breasts to his chest.

For just that instant, with Andres caught between deep tenderness and violent need, she was
the stronger one. And she felt the pulse of her
own strength, the certainty, the primitive heartbeat of ancient emotion. He was hers, he had
always been hers, and she was his; nothing in the
world would ever be as real as that.

Six

Sara wasn't aware of clothing falling away, only of the intimate shock of flesh meeting, burning and greedy. Their bodies strained to be closer, hard and demanding. Sara didn't know if he carried her to the bed or if she floated, didn't know which of them threw back the covers. It didn't matter.

She hadn't known what to expect of Andres as a lover. She knew the tenderness of his love and had glimpsed the strength of his passion, but nothing had prepared her for the astonishing depth of his ability to give of himself. He hid nothing, held back nothing. She had never felt so loved in her life.

He murmured endearments in English and Spanish as he loved her, his caresses achingly sensitive. In the soft light of the bedside lamp, he looked at her as if something of inestimable beauty and wonder had been given to him. He couldn't stop kissing her, couldn't stop touching heated, quivering flesh.

"Do you know what you do to me?" he murmured in a raspy voice, the warmth of his breath teasing even as his tone compelled. His lips lightly brushed a nipple hardened with wanting him, and his big hands slowly slid up her narrow waist until the swelling fullness of her breasts was captured.

Sara caught her breath, her nails digging into his shoulders. "I—I know what you do to me," she whispered, hardly recognizing her own voice.

His mouth brushed her straining flesh again and again, and his voice was rough, wondering. "From the first moment I saw you," he said, "I knew I was lost, lost somewhere in your lovely green eyes. I couldn't think, couldn't see anything but you. I was shaking inside, terrified some other man had found you before me and won your heart."

Andres's head lifted suddenly, and his eyes glittered with dark fire, with something implacable. "I would have done anything to win your love," he said fiercely. "Anything—" His voice caught, cracked. "Anything except hurt you or frighten you. I never wanted to do that, Sara."

"I know." She could barely get the words out through the tightness of her throat. "I know, Andres. It's all right now. Everything's all right now."

He groaned suddenly and buried his face between her breasts. "You make me drunk," he said tautly. "Make me crazy. *Dios*, Sara, I love you!"

Sara felt it then, felt the full force of his passion, his desire for her. It had been growing, building beneath the slow, gentle caresses, but now it swept over them both. His gentleness became driven hunger, urgent need. His big body was hard, burning, shaking with the force of his passion.

But this time, unlike that night in the garden, Sara didn't feel battered or bewildered by the sheer power of his desire. This time she felt a stunning force of her own rise within her, matching his. Fearless, exultant, she met need with need.

She felt his mouth at her breast, felt the swirling, maddening pleasure of his tongue. She felt the sure, insistent touch of his hand, felt her body yield as her legs parted for him. A moan caught in her throat and escaped raggedly when he found the warmth of her. The sensations were incredible, stealing her breath, shaking her body and soul.

Andres fought to master his body, to control the violence of his need, and it was the hardest thing he'd ever attempted in his life. She was so beautiful, so utterly responsive, and he ached because of needing her for so long. He heard a sound escape from somewhere deep inside him, wild with longing, and knew that never, as long as he lived, would his need of her lessen.

"Sara . . ."

The soft sounds she made ran through him like fire, and he could feel the last threads of his control snapping. Her slender body warm and yearning, ready for him.

"Andres, please!" Her voice was nearly gone, the faint, husky sound of limits reached, passed.

He widened her thighs gently and slipped between them, bracing himself above her. Sara looked up at him, dazed, aching; her hands found his shoulders, fingers compulsively probing smooth bronze skin and hard muscles.

"I love you," he said, his voice rough. "Sara . . ."

She felt a touch against her aching flesh, a pressure, then some instinct drove her to move suddenly, arching upward to meet him; she possessed even as he did. A cry of surprise caught in her throat, and her eyes widened with shock and pleasure. She thought his hot, dark eyes flickered briefly, flared with a new emotion, but there was no time to think about that.

Her supple limbs held him, her body sheathing his with tight heat, her passion meeting his wildly. She caught his rhythm, matched it in feverish response. She was driven, taking and giving, a shattering tension coiling until there was nothing but the primitive need to meld with him, to become a part of him until they were one.

The breathless, rushing tension snared them, tore at them, lifted them higher and higher until there was nothing to do but fall or fly, and they soared together in a sweeping ascent that was violent and tender and devastating.

Sara was slow in returning from that wondrous flight. Too utterly limp and drained to move, she was only vaguely aware that Andres had eased over beside her. But she felt his arms drawing her close, felt shaking hands stroke her hair, her body, as if he couldn't stop touching her. She found the strength somewhere to cuddle closer to the hard heat of his body, murmuring a wordless contentment.

She drifted, her entire body still tingling, pulsing slowly in a lazy heartbeat of pleasure. And if it occurred to her that she had burned all her bridges except the one between her and Andres, the thought didn't trouble her.

She didn't want to go back.

Colonel Durant sipped his wine and looked up from contemplating his half-finished dinner as Maria came into the room.

A little worried, the housekeeper said, "He went to find her hours ago, Colonel. Do you think . . ." Maria glanced toward the dining room door, speculation written large on her pleasant face. "Dinner is cold," she said almost absently. "They should eat."

"I imagine they will. When it occurs to them." Durant smiled. "Leave the food in a warm oven, Maria. If they wish to eat, they will."

The housekeeper was smiling, her button-like eyes bright. "It is good for them to reach the bedroom at last," she said happily. "I worried about them."

Durant didn't comment, but after Maria had returned to her kitchen, he sat brooding. He agreed with Maria; it *was* good that Andres and Sara had apparently taken the logical and vital next step in their relationship. It was good for both of them, he thought. He could almost literally feel an easing of tension in the house.

Still . . . He knew Andres well. And he knew his friend was deeply troubled by the uncertainty of the life he could offer the woman he loved here on Kadeira. Andres was well and truly caught, needing Sara desperately and yet also needing to know she would always be safe. And the latter was little short of impossible. Given time to think it through, Durant had the uneasy suspicion that Andres would, in the end, try to send her away.

Durant could understand, and he wondered what Sara's reaction would be. Did she know, he wondered, what she really meant to Andres? Did she comprehend what the depth of her own commitment would have to be? And if she did know and understand, was she willing to face the future at Andres's side? Could she persuade the man who loved her beyond all else to allow her that place in his life despite the dangers?

The colonel muttered a curse and drained his glass, barely tasting the wine. He wondered grimly if Andres had told her what they meant to do in the morning. Somehow he doubted it. But if Sara loved Andres as she said she did, the morning would bring a test of her ability to love in the face of danger.

Durant hoped she passed the test. For all their sakes.

Faint, years-old scars of a whip marked his back.

Sara had meant to slide from the bed and go downstairs in search of food, having been awakened by the complaints of her empty stomach. But she went still the moment she sat up, staring down at that wide, strong bronze back. He was lying on his stomach beside her, asleep, the covers having fallen to his hips when she sat up. And thin white lines crisscrossed from shoulders to waist, the marks of a cruel beating.

She reached out to trace the scars with soft

fingers, her throat aching. Her heart aching. So much pain . . .

"It was long ago," he said gently, raising up on one elbow to gaze at her with glowing eyes.

Sara eased back down onto her pillow, looking at him somberly. He slept like a cat, she thought. Or like a soldier. She wondered how many years it had been since he had been able to relax that constant guarded awareness. "What happened?" she asked.

Andres brushed a strand of her flaming hair away from her face, then stroked her cheek as if he couldn't stop touching her. "I was taken by the revolutionary army when I was fourteen," he murmured. "I had no choice. Kadeira's leader at that time had lasted longer in power than any other. Years. He was cruel; the rebellion against him was gaining strength. But the revolutionary leaders were little better than he was. They took children for their army, stole them from their homes in the dead of night."

"Is that how they got you?"

"Yes. My father had been killed before I was born—in an earlier revolution. My mother was killed a year after they took me, dying in a vicious raid on the town. I was one of the raiders."

Sara caught her breath. "Andres!"

His smiled twisted and his eyes went distant. "I didn't even know what we were doing. Few of us did. We had learned to do as we were told. I suppose the generals intended to kill only the government soldiers patrolling the town, but— It was a tragedy, Sara. So many were killed. There were looting and burning, terrible atrocities. By the time the government gathered its forces and drove us into the hills, there wasn't much left. The people could no longer stomach their *bright* revolution."

"What happened?" she whispered.

He sighed. "The so-called freedom fighters were weary too. Within a week the revolutionary army had been cut in half by desertions. Those of us who were left were mostly children with nowhere to go, our homes destroyed, families gone or having disowned us. Kadeira's leader took note, organized his army to round us up and capture us."

Sara was afraid to ask another question.

Tonelessly Andres said, "He meant to discourage future uprisings. We were thrown into his prison, and every day a dozen were taken to the center of town. Public whippings. Some of them fatal. The prisoners were left at the whipping posts from dawn until sunset, then were cut down. If they survived, they were free to rebuild their lives."

"You were just a boy!" Sara burst out. "How could—"

"I had carried a gun for a year, Sara," he said softly. "I wasn't a child any longer. I had fought like a man. I was punished like a man."

"No. Like—like an animal." She shook her head. "It wasn't right."

"There wasn't a right or a wrong then, my love. There was just the way things were."

After a moment Sara asked, "What did you do?"

"I survived." His faint smile attempted to soften the bleak words. "I found work at the docks. That was when I met John Chantry."

"The American mercenary? You've mentioned him before."

Andres nodded. "He changed my life. There were a number of mercenaries in the government's army; he was one. I don't know, to this day, what he saw in me, why he spent time with me." Andres laughed softly. "I was half wild, uneducated, filled with hate. But he fascinated me, because he was so much more than a soldier. He was quiet, thoughtful, intelligent. He read books and studied people, and no matter what had happened, he had never lost the belief that the world could be a good place."

"He taught you English?"

"Yes. And taught me to read; I had spent little time in school and could barely write my name when we met. He found books, borrowed or bought them from other soldiers and from the ships that occasionally came to Kadeira. He taught me to respect words and learning. And when I spoke bitterly of the government and of the unlikelihood of change, he was the one who told me that in every revolution there was one man with a vision. If the vision was good and strong, he said, the revolution would be successful. I never forgot that."

"Did he just leave one day?"

Andres shook his head slightly. "No. It was several years before revolution broke out again. The government was bleeding Kadeira dry; the people were being crushed under a merciless regime. I joined then, willingly. I wanted to fight the wrongness of it. John was making plans to leave; his contract had expired and he wasn't willing to fight any longer. He said he was getting old, that he wanted to go home.

"He never got the chance. In our first battle against government troops, I—I made something of a name for myself. Word reached the government, of course. The president was furious, and since he couldn't take his fury out on me, he took it out on John. Had him executed for collusion with enemies of the state. By the time I heard, it was all over."

Sara went into his arms silently, aching inside. What gave a man such strength? How had he kept going, year after year, with so much pain and loss, so much tragedy? And then she looked past his shoulder at the painting on the wall and she knew. Because he had a vision.

"Enough about the past," Andres said roughly. He pressed a trail of heated kisses from her trembling lips down her throat, over her breastbone. His hands caressed slowly. "It doesn't matter now. Nothing matters but this."

And for a while nothing did.

It was Andres who went down to the kitchen sometime after midnight and brought up a tray of food for them. And Sara discovered a new Andres in the lamplit quiet of the bedroom, a man of teasing humor, a man who seemed determined to close out the world, the past, the future. They were alone and in love.

And it wasn't until the dark hours before dawn, when she woke to the building fire of his renewed need, that Sara sensed a kind of desperation in him. He was silent expect for words of love murmured in a strained voice. His face was fixed, his eyes intense. He seemed driven to love her, as if some terrible premonition had warned him he would never again have the chance. And Sara, her own desire ignited, caught his urgent mood, responding with a half-bewildered intensity, a frantic need to soothe the hunger in his soul.

When it was over, there were no words. But Sara held on to him even as his arms cradled her, a nameless fear shadowing her mind and heart as her sated body relaxed in sleep.

Sara woke alone. The room was darkened; it wasn't yet dawn. Cold, she slipped from the bed, donned her shorts, and with no hesitation, one of Andres's shirts. She went out into the dimly lit hallway and then downstairs, drawn to the half-closed door of his office, where light spilled out.

She got as far as the door when the conversation between Andres and Colonel Durant stopped her. Listening, she went cold, colder than ever before in her life, and only her gritted teeth kept back the cry of protest screaming shrilly in her mind.

No! Not yet! I'm not ready to face this yet. . . .

"The men?" Andres asked, his voice remote.

"Waiting out front," the colonel answered, sounding worried. "Andres, I should be with you—"

"No. If something happens, I want you here, to take care of Sara."

Durant swore explosively. "Wait another day, then. To be certain, Andres. We can send in scouts, use their information to pinpoint Lucio's camp more precisely. We can throw every man we've got against—"

"And watch him fade away into the jungle the moment his own scouts hear us coming and report to him? Vincente, you know as well as I do that there's no possibility of approaching Lucio in that way. We've tried before. Our best chance is with this small group of our best jungle fighters attacking his camp before dawn."

"You'll be outnumbered by at least four to one," Durant reminded him grimly.

"I'll take those odds." Andre's voice held the sound of absolute finality.

Durant wouldn't give it up. "And if we're wrong? If Lucio has shifted his camp again? And if he's expecting you to come? If he has left his men scattered through the jungle waiting for you? You won't have a chance!"

Andres sighed. "Vincente, I don't have a *choice.* You know that as well as I do. Sara is in greater danger with every passing day."

"You can protect her here—"

"Can I? They took her from me once."

"A mischance! It couldn't happen again."

"Give me a guarantee!"

There was a moment of silence, thick and tense.

"I won't gamble her life on less than a guarantee," Andres said more quietly. "I must be sure. Go out and see to the men, Colonel; make certain they have everything we'll need."

After a moment Durant strode from the room, his jaw hard. He hesitated when he saw Sara outside the door, seemed about to speak, and then continued purposefully toward the front door without saying anything to her.

Sara remained where she was for long minutes. It hurt to breathe, and her throat ached. She was cold, so cold, and the thought of her life without Andres in it was an icy, black emptiness.

He was a target; she'd known that. But she hadn't expected him to stride willingly and determinedly into terrible danger. He had an *army*; why couldn't he send them instead of— But she knew. He'd never send his men where he refused to go himself. He would lead the way, just as he'd been born to do, just as his life had shaped him to do.

And she had to live with that.

He looked up, warned of her presence by instinct or the peculiar affinity between them rather than sound, for she made no noise. Slowly he slipped the big automatic into the webbed holster on his hip, half turning from the desk to face her. She looked so fragile, one of his shirts enveloping her, her long legs appearing to be bare. Her glorious hair was mussed, her eyes huge and unbelievably green.

His love for her swept over him, almost numbing in its intensity. It caught in his throat, knotted his stomach, dizzied his mind. He needed her with everything inside him—and with everything inside him, he needed the certainty of her safety. It was a knife in his heart.

"You should be sleeping," he murmured huskily. "The sun won't be up for hours yet."

She came toward him slowly, with the grace of music, stopping a bare step away. "I woke up alone," she said very softly. "I don't ever want to do that again."

Andres didn't touch her. He was afraid to touch her, afraid he'd never be able to leave her in order to do what had to be done. He felt his jaw aching and knew his teeth were clamped together to hold back what he felt, as if there were a dam some-

where inside him and it was a treacherously unsteady thing. "I'll be back within a few hours," he
said evenly.

"You're going after Lucio." It wasn't a question.

"We'll have no peace until he's defeated, Sara.
You know that."

She lifted her chin a little, something like reso-
lution flashing in her splendid eyes. "It has to be
today?"

"We have a good idea where his camp is. If we
delay, he could move again."

"I'm . . . a danger to you." She said it softly.

He reached out then, gathering her into his
arms and holding her tightly. She felt so fragile
against him, yet he knew the strength in her, the
passion. And he held on fiercely to the finest thing
in his life. "My love," he murmured into her silky
hair. "Without you, I don't think I could go on."

She drew back just far enough to look up at
him, her delicate face strained, her eyes wondering. "Your dream."

He smiled a little. "Even dreams wear out. Year
after year they seem farther beyond our reach. I'm
not a cat or a king, Sara; I can't walk alone. Not
any longer. I love you. And I need you beside me."

Their voices were low, words spoken with the
steady calm of something desperately important.
They could both hear, were painfully aware of the
merciless ticking of his wristwatch, loud in the
stillness of predawn, in the quiet of the room.
They both knew he had to leave, and soon.

Sara reached up to touch his cheek gently, feeling the tension in him. She didn't look down at
the gun he wore, or at the military starkness of
his dark uniform. She just looked at his face,

even though it had been fixed in her mind and heart long ago. "I'll be waiting when you get back," she said. "I love you, Andres."

He bent his head to kiss her, a deep, melding lover's kiss, then forced himself to release her. At the door he looked back for a long moment. She was leaning against the desk, watching him gravely. If he could keep her safe . . . if only he could keep her safe.

He left to join his men.

"I thought you might like coffee," Colonel Durant said.

"Thank you." Sara accepted the cup, sipped gratefully. She had gone upstairs to shower and dress after Andres had left, returning to the office minutes ago. Now she stood by the window, staring out at the slowly lightening sky.

Aware that Durant had settled into a chair near the desk behind her, she realized she needed badly to talk, to listen, to pass the time. She said suddenly, "It's odd. I always forget I'm a foreigner here. Andres makes me forget this isn't my country. As if it doesn't matter."

"Does it matter?"

She half turned to look at him, leaning back against the window frame. "To me? No. To him?"

"No," the colonel said, "not to him." And then, a little roughly, he added, "He'll be back, Sara. He has more lives than a cat."

"Does he?" Her voice was soft. "How many of those lives has he used up during the last twenty years or so?"

The question had no answer, and Durant didn't

offer one. After a moment he asked bluntly, "Can you handle this?"

"I'll have to, won't I?"

He studied her face. She was a little pale, her eyes darkened with shadows. But those eyes were direct and level, and her delicate mouth was held firmly. He never had been able to guess her thoughts, not like Andres did. Slowly he said, "This is Andres's life. It may get better; it will likely get worse at times. If you can't handle it, Sara, it would be a kindness to you both to end your relationship."

She smiled, not offended or angry but calmly reflective. "No. You see, Vincente, that's what I finally realized. This bond between us exists. We can't change it; we can't break it. It's stronger than we are. All we can do is fight to live with it." She drew a deep breath. "And that's why I'll handle this. Because I don't have a choice. I love him."

He nodded faintly, compassion and wonder stirring in his eyes. "Yes. I understand."

"Do you approve?" she asked.

"Do you need my approval?"

"No. Just curious."

"Then, yes, I approve. You brought something to Andres, gave back something he had lost. No man should be . . . too alone. He needs you." Durant hesitated, then said carefully, "He also needs to know you'll be safe. And you will never be as safe as he wants you to be on Kadeira."

"I know." Her voice was steady. "And he'll probably try to send me away. That's what you think, isn't it?"

"Yes." He didn't ask what she would do if Andres did indeed attempt to send her away to safety. He didn't have to ask now. Not any longer. He thought fleetingly and with rueful amusement that Andres just might, for the first time in his life, come up against someone who was more determined than he.

It was about time.

Lucio hadn't led his own soldiers into battle. He had expected Andres to move soon, and so had left only the shell of his most recent camp behind— along with a small number of his men. He was accustomed to moving, having learned bitterly that his old friend wouldn't allow him to grow complacent. He had survived all these years, had survived to fight steadily, but he found no comfort in the thought.

He was tired of it, tired of feeling like a hunted animal. He hated the constant stinking damp of the jungle, hated the years-old game of cat and mouse. And, most of all, he hated with all his soul the inescapable knowledge that Andres was the better general.

It galled him, feeding his hatred. Andres had not won—but neither had he lost. With the tenacity of apparently limitless strength, he kept coming, ignoring his enemy's elusiveness. Again and again, just as Lucio was pondering some lightning strike at his enemy, Andres would strike instead. And even though the battles were rarely conclusive, gaining Andres nothing, they served to keep Lucio off balance and on the run.

Just as it was now. Lucio knew that Andres's efforts would increase in intensity, since his woman was on Kadeira. Lucio knew Andres. So he had gathered the majority of his men and moved once more, fading into the jungle. He left some men at the camp, and some stationed in a loose perimeter around the almost deserted site.

What shook Lucio, and badly, though he didn't show it, was the fact that his men had traveled barely a mile from the old camp when they heard the gunfire behind them. A dawn attack. He didn't know if his own instincts were weakening, or if Andres's were getting stronger. He knew only that it was past time for a final, decisive battle.

His hatred washed over him then in a bitter, curdling wave. He had once wanted only victory, only himself in Andres's place as president of Kadeira; but that was no longer his true ambition. With every day that passed, his desire to break his old friend grew stronger. Break him in body, certainly. Even more, break his mind and his spirit. And for that Lucio needed Sara Marsh.

With the chattering of guns still echoing in the jungle a mile away, Lucio called several of his best men together and, by the light of a small fire, gave them the details of his plan.

Sara heard the gunfire. She tensed but said nothing to Colonel Durant. They were still in the office, both silent, waiting, because there was nothing else they could do. Durant was smoking cigarettes, the first time she'd seen him do that; she didn't comment. She almost asked for one herself but instead stood gazing out the window.

"How many men does he have?" she asked suddenly.

"Lucio?" Durant sounded tense. "In his camp at any one time, he usually has fifty or so. In his army, only God knows. We estimate from a hundred to two hundred."

"And Andres?"

"With him right now he has a dozen men," Durant answered flatly.

Sara leaned her forehead against the glass of the windowpane. Childhood prayers rose in her mind, as they had from the moment Andres had left, and she repeated them silently. She also added a few in her own words.

The sleek Learjet was descending toward a predawn Miami. The interior, efficiently soundproofed, was relatively quiet. None of those aboard were sleeping, though all were peaceful.

Raven studied them almost absently. Zach and Teddy were having a murmured discussion, and Raven didn't have to listen to know that he was doing his best to convince her to journey to Kadeira on the *Corsair* rather than the jet helicopter that had been sent ahead to Trinidad. He could command most people when he set his mind to it, even Josh on occasion, but Zach fought a losing battle when it came to his petite and hotly intrepid wife, Raven thought with amusement.

Derek and Shannon were aft; he was familiarizing himself with a large map of Kadeira while she sat close by and divided her attention between the map and her husband. Raven reflected happily on the fact that Shannon had lost the wounded look in her eyes since her marriage to Derek. She was still shy, still quiet, but she was gaining confidence every day. As for Derek, Raven had noticed that his hard, handsome face had softened somewhat, and he was quicker to smile.

Kelsey appeared to be dozing, although Raven knew he was awake and alert. Old habits die hard, and Kelsey had learned years ago to preserve his energy for future need. Probably he was thinking of Elizabeth, back home in Pinnacle and six weeks into a healthy pregnancy.

Thinking of Kelsey's happiness about that, Raven felt a pang. She and Josh were hoping; for months now they'd been trying. The doctor said everything was fine, not to worry, to be patient, but . . . They both wanted children. And they had seen both the joy and the heartache: Rafferty and Sarah had a healthy son, and Zach and Teddy had lost their unborn child.

Don't think past the assignment, she thought, scolding herself, as she'd often done in the past during difficult situations. This "assignment," of course, was of her own doing. Still . . . They would set down in Miami to await the photos scheduled to be taken later that day, thanks to General Ramsey's willing cooperation, and which would be delivered to them from the air force base. Then they'd lift off again, heading for Trinidad—assuming, of course, that the surveillance photos convinced them there were no antiaircraft guns on Kadeira.

Both the jet helicopter and the *Corsair* were waiting in Trinidad. It had been more or less decided that Zach, Josh, Derek, Kelsey, and she would go into Kadeira on the helicopter. Teddy was in the process of perhaps being persuaded by Zach to join Shannon on the *Corsair*, which would make a more leisurely—and probably safer—trip to the island. If Lucas and Kyle, delayed in Washington, could reach Trinidad in time, they, too, would be on the yacht.

They planned to contact President Sereno via radio just minutes before the helicopter reached Kadeira; visitors arriving by air on Kadeira were distinctly rare, and all of them had agreed it would be best to give Sereno time to alert his soldiers they weren't being attacked.

Raven heard a click beside her and turned to look at her husband as Josh closed his briefcase. She lifted a brow questioningly.

Josh laid the case aside. "Possible," he told his wife quietly, in answer to the silent question. "It'll mean a hell of a lot of legal maneuvering, possible flak from the U.S. government, and it'll take time."

"What did Derek say?" she asked.

"He wants in—if we can minimize the risk. And that's the question, of course. We could put together a group of investors within a matter of days, but they'd want safety guarantees, and that just isn't possible." He sighed, then smiled at his wife, his hard blue eyes softening. "Hell, I can call in a few favors and avoid government hassles; on our end the rest will be easy. Derek and I've agreed to put the proposal to Sereno. If we can make progress, then we can nose around and find some other investors."

"If Sereno can keep Kadeira stable," Raven said.

Josh nodded. "And that's the rub. Assuming Sereno agrees, *and* assuming Lucio can be put out of action, our best chance is to move as quickly as possible. And there are risks with that. Sereno will have to hold his government with an iron fist when money starts to pour into the economy; too much will be as bad as too little, unless he handles it just right."

Softly Raven said, "You're putting a lot of faith in him."

Smiling, Josh said, "I believe it's justified." He took his wife's hand in his. "We'll see, won't we?"

Raven was silent for a moment, then said, "This began as a mission to rescue a kidnapped woman; now we're going in to try to patch the wounds of an injured country. You don't believe Sara will want to leave, do you?"

Josh shook his head slightly. "No. I met the man, and I can tell you, he's plenty persuasive. Lord knows it's no secret he loves her; there's a better than even chance she loves him. But it's like Shannon said. Whether or not they stay together, they should at least be able to settle it without a sword hanging over their heads."

Raven nodded. She heard the change in the engines that indicated they were landing. "We get the photos this afternoon?"

"Right. We can be in Kadeira by tomorrow afternoon."

Kelsey stirred and said plaintively, "And I didn't even bring my swimming trunks!"

Seven

The sun was coming up, and the distant gunfire was long since over when the sounds of vehicles could be heard approaching the house. Sara was out of the office and racing for the front door before Durant could move, but he was only a few steps behind her when she flung open the door and rushed outside.

The two jeeps that had taken Andres and his team partway to Lucio's camp were drawn up in front of the house. The men got out. Two bore superficial wounds but stood easily with little help and seemed more annoyed than in pain.

Andres was speaking to them when Sara first saw him—and he never got a chance to finish what he'd been saying. She threw herself into his arms, holding on fiercely, only dimly aware that the formerly morose men were now grinning and clapping each other on the back, as if they'd had a hand in their president's obviously successful courtship.

Sara didn't cry. The fear had gone too deep to find an easy expression of relief now. She just held on to the solid reality of his presence, the flesh-and-blood certainty. He was whole and unharmed. Safe—for now. It was enough.

Andres held her, lifting her off her feet briefly in a strong hug and then kissing her quickly. He kept an arm around her to guide her back to the house, saying something in Spanish over one shoulder to his men. They laughed.

"What did you say?" she asked, a little breathless from relief and the greeting.

His black eyes gleamed down at her. "That life rewarded the pure of heart," he told her solemnly.

Sara laughed despite her tangle of emotions. But then she sobered, remembering the earlier morose faces of his men. "You didn't get Lucio, did you?"

Andres walked beside her into the house, gesturing to a very obviously relieved Colonel Durant to accompany them into the office. He didn't answer until they were inside the room, then shrugged ruefully. "No, we didn't get him. From all the signs, he had moved out less than an hour before. There were a few of his men left behind; you probably heard the gunfire."

"Yes." Sara sat down on the arm of a chair and watched Andres move behind his desk and take off the gun belt he wore. "Two of your men were wounded. Did you . . . lose anyone?"

He shook his head. "No. But Lucio lost four of his men."

"Attrition." Durant, standing by the desk, sounded bitter. "He loses a few of his men, or we lose a few. But it changes nothing. And the war goes on."

"The war goes on," Andres agreed somberly.

Durant sighed explosively and said, "I'll go and see to the men, Andres."

When he had gone, Sara said, "He was worried to death about you." She drew a deep breath. "So was I."

Andres's smiled was crooked. "All for nothing—except that we know where Lucio *isn't*. At least for today."

"What now?"

"We try again." He looked at her steadily. "Tomorrow. Or the day after. We keep trying until we get him." He watched the effect of his words on her face, saw her eyes go dark briefly, her lips tighten. Then he saw her chin lift fractionally, and the green eyes glittered with a steely determination.

"Then that's what you do," she said calmly.

The knife in his heart twisted. He had known she had strength, and watching her discover it as well was both a fascination and a torment. She shouldn't have had to find out this way, he thought in pain. Not like this, in sudden danger and violence. An ordinary life would have tested her enough, with its daily triumphs and tragedies; the life he offered was one long ordeal without respite.

He didn't have the right to ask this of her.

"Andres?"

He looked at her, at the finest, most beautiful dream he had ever dreamed. Like the vision that had sent him to war, it seemed that fate intended to torture him with this dream, too, taunting him with what he could touch briefly but which would always have to be just beyond his reach.

"I love you," he said quietly.

She came to him, smiling a little, her eyes gentle and loving. "I love you too," she murmured. And then, her smile widening, she added, "Why don't we go back to bed for a few hours? President Sereno is entitled, isn't he?"

"Definitely." He swept her up into his arms, holding her easily as he started toward the stairs.

He felt the knife twist again but bore it stoically. For now she was his. In his arms, his bed, his life. Warming the coldness near his soul. Holding back the darkness that threatened always to overtake him.

The affinity between them, Sara had discovered, strengthened with every passing hour. She thought that perhaps their being lovers had intensified that bond; the potential of closeness had always been present, and the intimacy of a physical relationship had sealed the bond.

And there were times when she thought she could even read his thoughts. She knew, at any rate, what he was going through. She felt it in the fierceness of his lovemaking, saw it in the depths of his eyes, heard it in his voice. She couldn't make it easier for him, as much as she wanted to.

He loved her and needed her, but he would, in the end, try to send her away. She knew that. But she also knew now that there *was* a core of strength in her, an innate determination. She had fought too hard to love, to understand, to accept; she had learned how to fight.

She thought she had even learned during those fearful predawn hours how, if necessary, to fight him.

For the present she could only wait. Until Lucio was dealt with, there would be no talk of her leaving. She had no intention of pressing Andres on the point, but it still hurt her when he gazed at her in unguarded moments as if she were a dream, soon to turn to mist.

Love and pain. They seemed two halves of one.

That day was spent quietly. Maria served a late breakfast when Andres and Sara reappeared a few hours later; she beamed happily at both of them. Colonel Durant joined them for the meal, and he and Andres talked about finding Lucio and about other work that had to be seen to that day.

Sara left them to it after breakfast and spent some time in the garden with Carlos, remembering, this time, to wear a hat against the building heat of the day. She picked up a few new Spanish words from the gardener, amused to realize that her vocabulary was increasing with regard to roses and endearments, but nothing of a more practical nature.

Amused or not, she searched the library after lunch, finding at last an old and tattered Spanish grammar book and one Spanish-English dictionary. Andres found her curled up in a chair in the room hours later, engrossed in Spanish grammar and muttering softly to herself.

"What are you doing, *mi corazón*?" he asked curiously, half sitting on the arm of her chair and smiling down at her.

"I'm *trying* to learn Spanish—and my college French isn't helping me any," she replied ruefully.

He chuckled softly, taking the book from her

and looking at it. "This won't help much, either. You need to hear the language spoken aloud. If you're too impatient to learn from me, my love, we'll order cassettes—"

When he broke off abruptly, Sara knew that he was remembering his intention to send her away. Ignoring that, she rose up on her knees in the chair and slipped her arms around his neck. "I intend to learn a great deal from you," she said solemnly. "But I am impatient, darling, so—" The words were lost forever, because Andres kissed her suddenly; Sara didn't much care about his words, anyway, not when his actions were so wonderful.

He left her a few minutes later to return to his office, and Sara sat with the grammar book in her lap and stared into space. She found that although she could accept the danger of Andres's life with at least a semblance of composure, the nemesis that was Lucio roused in her a deep and unbearable resentment. He was *there*, hanging over their heads, haunting every thought like a specter.

Nothing could be decided until he was out of their lives; nothing could be settled. She couldn't confront Andres with her intention of remaining there because the threat to her from Lucio was so strongly fixed in Andres's mind that nothing she could say would overcome that.

She could only wait, wait and watch Andres look at her with haunted eyes. And for the first time in her life she found she could hate with an implacable certainty. She hated Lucio, hated him for what he was doing to Andres.

It wasn't until later in the evening when she was at his side and boneless in the aftermath of lovemaking that she asked Andres the question in curiosity.

"Do you hate Lucio?"

"Hate?" Andres was quiet for a few moments, one hand almost compulsively stroking her fiery hair. "Once I did."

"When?"

"Before I met you."

She lifted her head from his shoulder, looking at him gravely in the dim light from the bedside lamp. "Why? I mean, why did you hate him then but not now?"

"I hated him because of what he was doing to Kadeira. And I suppose I hated him because he hated me. When friendship turns to hate, it is a bitter thing. After I met you I saw it was a waste to hate when I could love. And love, no matter how painful, doesn't corrode the soul."

Sara thought about his words, realizing she had been right about her importance to Andres. And she wondered how many women were granted the knowledge that they were not only deeply loved but also deeply needed by the men who held their hearts. It was a humbling thought. She pulled herself up to kiss him, then asked softly, "What happened between you and Lucio? How did it go so wrong?"

"I don't know," he answered simply. "Oh, there were signs even before I gained power. Lucio was intolerant of any delay in carrying out a plan. He was convinced that force could move mountains, while guile and patience were useless. But I thought he believed, as I did, that change would take time and patience."

Andres was silent for a few moments, and Sara waited. After a time he went on quietly.

"It seemed, when the revolution was finally over, that Lucio was content. There was so much to do, so much work. We were both busy for months just discovering what there was to work with. Then, gradually, the discord between us grew. He pushed for execution of the government troops we had overthrown; I refused. He insisted we apply to communist governments that had shown an interest in constructing a military base here; I refused. He had dreams of Kadeira becoming an international scene for gambling; I had seen how gambling could destroy much more than it built, and I didn't want that for Kadeira.

"I intended to work toward a goal of free elections, a goal of democracy; he thought me weak for it. I wanted to persuade foreign businessmen to invest here; he complained that too many concessions would have to be granted. And, more than anything else, I wanted Kadeira to be content and at peace, prosperous for its people."

"And what did Lucio want?" she asked after a moment.

"Ultimately? He wanted power. He saw Kadeira as a stepping-stone to greater things."

"That's why you can't let him win."

"Yes. He would do what half a century of revolution has been unable to do: destroy Kadeira."

Sara moved even closer, resting her head on his shoulder again. "You won't let him. You'll stop him."

Andres didn't respond aloud. He held her, listened as her soft breathing gradually deepened into sleep, felt her warmth beside him. He wanted to hold on to her with all his strength, all his will, with every ounce of driven need. Instead he held her closely but gently.

She had asked about Lucio and about hate, still trying, he realized, to understand what she had accepted more or less on faith. She hadn't asked about the terrorists at all, and he knew she wouldn't; that, too, was accepted.

And she gave her own love without reservation, offering support and understanding, offering the warmth and light he craved. She was an utterly natural, totally responsive lover, uninhibited and delighted in his arms.

His beautiful love. *Caged.*

And not safe even in the cage. Surrounded by the fence and the guards, not safe. He had asked this of her, hoping it wouldn't matter, hoping she would be blind to fences and guards. And she seemed to be. Now. But there would always be some variation of a cage, and she would always, in necessity, be forced to live inside it with him.

But even then—never safe.

Andres's arms tightened, still gently, around her. He left the bedside lamp on even as sleep began to claim him, but it was her light and warmth he held close, wondering in pain if there would be anything left to hold the cold darkness at bay when she was gone.

A dawn raid on the town woke them.

By the time they had dressed quickly and hurried downstairs, even Sara knew that the raid on the town was no small skirmish. The sounds of guns were constant; there was the chatter of automatic weapons, the occasional *cra-aack* of high-powered rifles, and the hollow booming of shotguns as the townspeople fought the raiders. And, above the rest, the chilling violence of explosions as buildings were blasted into rubble.

Durant was in the office waiting for them, and the long-forbidden radio crackled and whined with the harried reports from those of Andres's men stationed in the town. And, even above the rest, they could hear the angry shouts and curses of the soldiers outside the house who were not involved in the battle.

Lucio had thrown his entire army against the town for the first time.

"The town and harbor patrols are outnumbered." Durant's voice was terse. "The ships' captains are moving their vessels out of the harbor to avoid mortar fire; they ask if you wish them to fire on the town."

"No." Andres's face was a mask, hard. "I won't sanction that. Guns from the ships would kill innocent citizens. Have the captains send every available man to the town; they can come ashore at the beach on the east side of the island."

Durant relayed the order, then looked at Andres. "It won't be enough," he said bleakly.

Sara's voice came steadily into the silence. "Almost a third of your men are guarding the house."

Andres looked at her, his face still hard but hell leaping at her out of his eyes. "It could well be a diversion," he said. "To get to you."

"That doesn't matter. You can't let them destroy the town."

She was right, and he knew it, had known it all along. But that didn't make his orders easier to give. He looked at his waiting colonel and spoke flatly. "Leave two men on the parapet, a dozen guarding the perimeter—but pull them inside the fence. Have the rest ready to go in ten minutes."

Durant saluted and strode quickly from the room.

"I'll stay here," Andres told Sara.

"No, you won't."

"Vincente can lead the men, Sara." He wasn't arguing, merely stating a fact.

"I know that. But they fight for you, Andres. For *you*. You always lead them, and that can't change now." It took all her control to say the words calmly, steadily. "We both know that. You have to go on fighting for your people."

"Sara . . ."

"I can't be allowed to change you!" she said fiercely. "You can't be less than you are. If I weren't here, you'd go with your men without hesitation, without even thinking about it. Wouldn't you?"

He didn't answer, just looked at her.

An explosion in the town made the floor shudder beneath their feet, and Sara drew a deep breath. "I know how to handle a gun, and I'm a good shot." She nodded toward the far wall, where he kept a small handgun collection. "I'll find something in there. Maria and I will go down into the cellar just in case, and stay there until you come back. We'll be fine, Andres."

After a moment Andres bent slowly and got his webbed holster from the desk drawer. He buckled the belt in place, then came around the desk and pulled her into his arms. "If anything happens to you—"

"Nothing will." She lost herself for a few precious heartbeats in the heat of his kiss, then found a smile from somewhere. "Just . . . come back to me."

"Always." And it was a vow chiseled in stone.

Sara went to the front door with him and watched the jeeps disappear into the slowly lightening darkness before closing and locking the door. She went to find Maria in the kitchen, telling the pale and quiet housekeeper that they were going to spend a few hours in the cellar. Grateful for something to do, Maria began gathering a few snacks and drinks to take with them.

Sara returned to the office and went to study the handguns in Andres's collection. Not allowing herself to think of anything but practical defense, she made a swift choice and took a Colt automatic from the case. The gun was cleaned and oiled, the clip holding seven bullets. Sara weighed the gun in her hand, then double-checked the safety and stuck the gun inside the waistband of her jeans.

She could indeed handle guns. Her father, a career army man who'd been undismayed by having a daughter rather than a son, had taught her from a young age to know and respect guns, to handle them easily, and to fire them well.

She had practiced regularly, especially during the past few years. While moving so constantly to avoid what she had thought had been Andres's men, she had practiced at various target ranges, renting a pistol rather than keeping her own. As much as she would have preferred a gun of her own during those hectic days, she had decided reluctantly against it; the police and the FBI took a dim view of guns carried across state lines, and she had been constantly on the move.

She had accepted then, somewhat to her shock, that in her own defense she could have shot at something other than a target. But that had not been put to the test then. Now it looked as though it would.

On the point of turning away from the gun case, Sara hesitated. What was it her father had once told her? That police officers often kept "backup" guns other than their service revolvers on the theory that one gun might jam or be lost, and another might be needed. And Sara had often muttered in disgust while reading of fictional heroines who had *known* they were in danger and hadn't taken the simplest precautions.

Sara hesitated, then went quickly upstairs to change her running shoes for a pair of soft-soled ankle boots. She returned to the gun case and removed a tiny derringer, studying it thoughtfully. Useless for any long-range defense, of course, but quite effective at close range. She made sure it was cleaned and loaded, then bent and slid the little gun into the top of her right boot. It was virtually hidden there, and yet she could get to it quickly if the need arose. It made a small but comforting weight against her ankle.

She hesitated yet again, forcing her mind to work methodically and trying to ignore the continuing sounds of gunfire and explosions from the town. Was there anything else she could do?

Lucio wanted to capture rather than kill her, wanted to use her to force Andres to renounce power. Wanted, even, to break his enemy thoroughly and completely.

Torture.

Sara felt the coldness of rational fear but tried to think practically. Ropes, perhaps. Ropes . . . She went to Andres's desk and rummaged for something vaguely remembered, emerging at last with a small, flat penknife. It wasn't much as knives went, but the blade was sharp, and it would be almost invisible in her hip pocket with the tail of her summer blouse loose over it. She thrust it into her pocket grimly.

She found Maria waiting for her at the top of the cellar steps, and it was only then that she remembered something.

"Damn. Oh, damn, and I'll bet— Maria, did Andres know how I got through the fence when I ran away before?"

Bewildered, the housekeeper said, "He was wild then, half crazy. Nobody knew how you got out, and he didn't blame anyone."

Sara was torn for a moment, knowing she had promised Andres to remain in the cellar. But . . . "Maria, go on into the cellar. I'm just going to speak to one of the guards outside."

She left the housekeeper worried and upset, then went quickly out through the kitchen and into the garden. It was almost light now, gray and misty, and Sara hadn't gone three steps before she encountered a young soldier who relaxed perceptibly when he realized who she was.

"*Señora . . .*"

He had her already married, Sara thought, and could hardly help but grin a little. "Do you speak English?" she asked him.

He looked blank, worried. Tried a hesitant "No."

"Damn." She had been a little tardy in worrying about speaking Spanish, Sara realized. If none of the guards here at the house spoke English, she'd have to do this herself. She felt, briefly, like a foreigner, then smiled ruefully at the soldier. "*De nada,*" she said, using one of the few phrases she knew.

He made an anxious sound when she continued on into the garden toward the western fence. "*Señora!*"

Sara waved a hand dismissively at him and went on, pushing through the shrubs rather than taking the path.

What with one thing and another, it hadn't occurred to her to ask Andres about the opening in his defenses that she'd discovered two years ago. She thought it had probably been closed by now just as a matter of course, but there was always a chance it hadn't, and a chance was too much.

When she got to the fence, she was relieved that she had remembered to check, because the gap was still there.

It wasn't really much of an opening, however. Rainwater had eroded a narrow gully that ran from just inside the fence all the way down the hill, leaving a gap of about two feet square between the bottom of the fence and the base of the gully. It wasn't an obvious opening, being almost completely hidden from inside the fence by a creeping shrub that had crept over most of the hole, and more or less invisible from outside the fence because more greenery practically hid the gully.

But it was an easy way in.

Sara paused for a moment, staring down at the gap. She'd have to go back toward the house and try to find a soldier who spoke English. Failing that, she'd just lead one of them there and make the problem obvious. She began to turn away, then realized something with a jolt of fear, and her hand was closing around the Colt's grip even before she was consciously aware of it.

The creeping shrub was flattened, its gleaming green leaves torn and mashed into the ground. The opening was obvious—because someone had already used it.

Someone was inside the fence.

Sara had an instant to reflect bitterly that she was no better than those stupid, unprepared fictional heroines. Made less wary by soldiers and her own guns, she had trotted out cheerfully to check on a breach in the defenses on her own instead of pulling up the drawbridge, flooding the moat, and barricading herself in the castle like any sensible heroine.

Her gun was in her hand, but she never got the chance to fire it. With only a fleeting awareness of someone behind her, Sara felt an explosion of pain in her head and crumpled to the ground without a sound.

Sara had underestimated the young soldier. He had been wretchedly aware of his inability to communicate with her and shuddered at the very thought of dragging the president's lady back to the house against her will, but seeing her roaming in the garden, armed or not, scared him to death. The moment she disappeared into the shrubbery, he raced quickly around the house until he found Captain Morales, who *did* speak English.

"Captain, the lady. She's in the garden."

Morales cursed bitterly, but he was moving at the same time, moving quickly and ordering the younger man to show him where the lady was.

The shooting started all around then, as one of

Andres's guards encountered one of Lucio's men—inside the fence. And there were, it developed, half a dozen of Lucio's men inside the perimeter. The small battle didn't last long, ending in minutes, with the enemy dead and two of Andres's men wounded.

But the lady was gone.

They found her gun near the fence, and it was obvious she had been taken out through the unsuspected opening. There was no sign of movement. Morales ordered his men to search the house and grounds, just in case, but he knew they were too late.

He would have to go to the president and tell him. He didn't look forward to that.

At some level of her mind Sara was still swearing at herself when she fuzzily came back to consciousness. She knew time had passed; not even the interlacing of jungle greenery above her head could block out the hot morning sun. And it was very hot, damp, and sticky.

With her eyes still half closed and unfocused, Sara silently took stock. She was sitting on the ground, her back and aching head against a narrow tree. Her wrists were bound with ropes—in front of her. She thought that was ironic and even amusing; after her careful selection of a knife with which to cut ropes, she couldn't get her hands around behind her to *get* it. Which certainly said something about best-laid plans. And since her ankles were tied as well, Sara wasn't sure she could get to her small derringer.

She forced her eyes to focus, studying her bound

ankles. She could, just barely, see the derringer's grip, and she didn't think the gun was inaccessible; it didn't feel as though those ropes were pressing it against her ankle, at any rate. So maybe she still had that ace. The problem was, she wouldn't know for sure until she tried—and any attempt would certainly give away the gun's hiding place.

Because he was watching her very closely.

Deliberately, perhaps unwilling to look death in the face, she turned her head slowly and gazed around at her surroundings instead. A jungle camp, mostly deserted. There were signs that a large number of men had been here at least a couple of days, but they were gone now, fighting in the town.

There were only two men present. One was a burly, bearded soldier with blank eyes. He stood a few yards away, holding a rifle. He wasn't looking at her but scanning the area almost automatically, and he held the rifle like a friend.

The other man . . .

He was slightly above medium height. Dark, of course. Slender to the point of thinness, but when he moved, it was obvious there were muscles. It was obvious there was strength and determination and purpose.

Sara hadn't wanted to look at his face. But she looked at last, compelled to know what she could about this man who would certainly kill her—after he made both her and Andres suffer.

He was standing only a couple of feet away from her, staring down at her. He was handsome in the way a glacier is beautiful: cold, remote, deadly. His black eyes were unusually large, unnaturally brilliant with cunning and something else. Evil. He had a wide, mobile mouth that was sensual and cruel. A mouth that smiled like the gates of hell.

Lucio.

Suddenly he spit a single word at her in Spanish, and Sara didn't have to understand the word to catch the meaning. He was, she realized in vague surprise, calling her a whore. She didn't know why that surprised her, except that she wouldn't have expected him to waste time with words. But then she began to wonder if he intended to break her mind and soul as well as her body, and looking into those brilliant, hate-filled eyes, she thought he just might.

She fought to keep her face expressionless, to keep command of her voice. "Sorry," she said ironically. "I'm afraid I don't speak Spanish."

He laughed. There was, astonishingly enough, a glint of real amusement in his eyes. And his wide, white smile remained. "You're Andres's woman," he said, his English as easy and idiomatic as Andres's, his voice deep and somewhat quick.

"You knew that before you grabbed me," she said.

His gaze flickered over her disordered hair, and his smile widened. "The only redhead on the island—I would hardly make a mistake about that." Then he stepped forward and calmly ripped her blouse open from top to bottom.

Eight

"Are you sure you want to do this?" Derek asked Josh through the headphones all of them were wearing. "We're dropping into a war zone."

Josh, piloting the jet helicopter that was descending rapidly toward a clearing in front of the stucco house, sent a glance toward the town, noted the rising smoke, the signs of fires burning all over the place. A war zone, indeed. "Durant didn't say no," he reminded Derek.

Raven leaned forward from her place in back and said somewhat dryly, "Didn't say yes, either. Not exactly. Roughly translated, he said something along the lines of 'Oh, hell.' He sounded a bit upset."

Zach, who had been cursing more or less steadily since they'd first seen what was happening on Kadeira, interrupted his own swearing to say, "Lucio must have thrown his entire army against the town."

Kelsey, who was sitting by the rear door and looking out, asked suddenly, "Why didn't Sereno answer the radio call?"

"Dammit," Josh said after a moment, and then concentrated on setting the big jet helicopter down as near as possible to the house.

They had made good time from Trinidad, arriving hours earlier than they had expected. And the radio call to alert Sereno, placed just minutes ago, had garnered a most unsatisfactory response. Colonel Durant had answered, saying only briefly that the president wasn't available and warning them that the government wouldn't be responsible for their safety.

Still, the soldiers near the house had drawn back to give the helicopter room to land, and on those tired, grimy faces were expressions of only faint curiosity. They had obviously been alerted about the arrival. None took up a defensive stance, and none tried to stop them when they left the aircraft.

Durant was waiting for them at the front door, and though Kelsey was the only one he knew by sight, he quickly singled out Josh after a faintly surprised glance at Raven. "You're taking quite a risk, Mr. Long," he said in a voice that contained, more than anything else, weariness.

"Our risk to take," Josh noted dryly, and quickly introduced the others. "I gather Lucio attacked the town?" he asked when the colonel had acknowledged the introductions.

Durant nodded, unsurprised by their apparent knowledge, and stepped back to allow them into the house. "This way." He led them toward Andres's office. "Lucio has gone berserk," he told them, still tired. "He threw all his men in a suicide raid against the town. Even the townspeople fought them. He no longer has an army."

"The revolution?" Raven ventured.

Durant shrugged, hardly the picture of triumph. "Over. But it doesn't matter now. He'll be president before nightfall."

"Sara," Derek said softly.

Durant didn't answer; he didn't have to. As they entered the office they all heard Sereno's voice, a voice beyond weariness, beyond pain and fear; a numb voice.

"Vincente, try to raise him again."

Durant went toward the radio but said, "He won't answer. He'll talk when he's ready, and not before."

"Try."

The newcomers stood inside the office and gazed at the president of Kadeira. He was leaning back against his desk, his face gray and blank, seemingly unaware of the young doctor who was working quickly to bandage a wound high on his left arm. His dark uniform was torn in a couple of places and smelled of smoke; his face, like his soldiers', was grimy and drawn with weariness; like his colonel, he showed no triumph.

He looked at them finally, seemed to focus on them at least a little. Mildly, almost conversationally, he said, "This is not a good time to visit."

Josh's first thought was, God, he's like Zach. And he knew that was true, even though he had missed it years before when he had first met Sereno. He had missed it, and that told him this man had amazing control that would not be broken easily, yet was now in splinters.

And heaven help Lucio, Josh thought. Because Sereno, like Zach, would act out of rage on occasions so rare they could be counted on one hand during a lifetime. And during those thankfully rare occasions he would be a human earthquake, a one-man army, death on the prowl.

A primitive force beyond civilized bounds.

Josh thought the man was very likely beyond reach, but he tried, and he used all the experience gained in more than fifteen years of knowing Zach; he looked into eyes that were windows to hell, and he didn't waste time. "We might be able to help," he told Sereno calmly.

The president continued to look at him without interest, without, really, very much attention at all. "He has Sara." A quiver disturbed the blankness of his expression. "He took her from me again."

Raven left the others to move forward until she stood directly in front of Sereno. "We care about Sara too," she said quietly, gently. "Let us help."

Sereno looked at her, and it seemed that he saw her, that something in her was reaching him. Perhaps it was her voice. Perhaps it was the steady calm in her violet eyes. Whatever it was, it seemed to touch a cord of response. With a smile that was no more than a bleak curve of his lips, he said, "I've never asked for help before."

"Then it's time you learned to do so," Josh said flatly.

The black eyes swung his way, seemed to focus. This time there was faint interest. "Yes."

Sara hadn't worn a bra. She wished now that

she had, although he probably would have torn that as well. With an effort that went against every instinct, she didn't try to fight him, made no effort to lift her bound hands and hold him off. She just sat there and stared up at him. And it wasn't his gaze she felt crawling like a chill over her bare breasts, but the other man's, the soldier's. He had stepped closer instantly, his greedy eyes fixed on her with lewd interest.

Lucio looked down at her for a moment, at her face rather than her breasts, then twitched the shirt back into place so that it more or less concealed her breasts again. He straightened and rapped out a sharp command to the soldier.

His face wiped of all expression but his eyes still hot, the soldier turned his back and walked a few steps away.

"Andres's woman." Lucio laughed but seemed oddly satisfied. "I should have known he'd choose one with pride." He studied her for a moment with assessing eyes, then leaned over again and slapped her.

Sara felt the pain of the flat, open-handed blow as it rocked her head, but it was the primitive, soul-deep shock of it that dizzied her. No man had ever hit her like that, a blow meant to degrade and humiliate more than hurt. It was a cool use of male strength, a sure gesture of domination. She tasted blood and didn't make a sound. Slowly she fixed her eyes on his face again and lifted her chin. And she wondered how long she could hold out against his kind of calm cruelty.

Not long. Not long at all.

"Ah." Lucio nodded as if some private deduction had been confirmed. "Strength as well. Good. You'll break slowly, then. Excellent for my purpose."

"And that is?" she asked, knowing.

"To break Andres, of course," he said conversationally. He gestured to a silent radio set on a rickety table nearby. "He's no doubt calling me now, willing to offer anything for your safe return. But I don't ask anything. *I ask everything.* I will break him until there's nothing left of him."

"You won't." She was thinking of nothing, just the need to hold on, to gain time. . . . Anything to avert this planned destruction of the man she loved.

He chuckled. "No? Oh, I think so. I have a tape recorder I'll get in just a few moments. It will be delivered to Andres in due time. A message. He'll hear me break you, slowly, and it will break him."

She half shook her head. "He'll kill you."

Lucio was still amused. Horribly amused. "Cripples don't kill, my dear. And he'll be a cripple by the time I've finished with you."

"What are you going to do?" She hadn't wanted to ask the question, but it emerged on its own, a product of her instinctively shrinking mind.

"I'll take you first." His voice was chillingly calm and thoughtful. "Take Andres's woman. I'll tell him what I'm doing, of course, and you'll tell him as well."

Her body was cold, her throat tight. "No. I won't."

"Yes, you will. It's amazing what a human being will do just to live for a few more minutes. You'll be surprised." He said it as if he were offering an interesting experience. "You'll find yourself doing just as I demand. You'll hear yourself beg for more time. For life. You will actually be aware of the disintegration of your mind, and you'll feel the tears come from a place you never knew existed inside you."

If there had been anything in Sara's stomach, she would have thrown up; as it was, she had to choke back the bitter bile rising in her throat. Evil. Only a mind of pure evil could conceive of, and casually discuss with an intended victim, the utter destruction of a fellow human being.

"You've gone white, my dear." His voice was solicitous, just as a hangman's would be when he asked politely if the rope was too tight. Not to worry; you won't feel a thing in a moment. Not a thing.

Sara swallowed hard.

"It isn't so easy to be strong, is it?" He was mocking her, speaking in a gentle tone and with spurious sympathy. "Theory is one thing, reality is something else again. Just think of it. After I've had you, Sabin over there will fetch his whip. He hasn't had a lovely female body to mark in a long time; he'll enjoy it very much. He won't beat you to death, of course; that would be too quick. He'll beat you until you scream without stopping for breath."

That wouldn't, Sara thought, be very far off. The screams were, even now, crawling around in her mind, her throat, behind locked teeth. But she kept them trapped there. She didn't feel brave or strong; she felt sick and terrified. But her voice, to her dim astonishment, emerged calmly. "You think you know Andres, think you know what he'll do. But you're wrong. You might use me to beat him—but you won't break him. He's worth a hundred of you, and you won't break him."

Lucio sneered. "The voice of love."

Sara leaned her head back against the tree and conjured a smile full of all the mockery she could muster. "You think you know that, too, but you're wrong. It isn't love—it's fact. Men like Andres don't break. It's men like you who do, hollow men with nothing but hate holding them together."

Lucio smiled, but it was a tight, dangerous smile. "We shall see, my dear."

Sara was afraid he was right about that. Very afraid.

"A reconnaissance plane took this yesterday afternoon," Zach said tersely, placing a large photograph on Andres Sereno's desk. "It shows a fair-sized concentration of people in the jungle—here."

Andres leaned over to study the photo, frowning. "Lucio's abandoned camp was farther to the east."

"Could they have been your men?" Josh asked him.

"No. I was concerned with protecting the town and this house—for all the good it did." Andres's mouth twisted a bit.

Zach, the only one other than Andres with military experience, could have pointed out that—barring Sara—it had actually been a good tactical idea. Lucio had been forced to throw his entire army against the town and consequently had been defeated. Except, of course, that there *was* Sara; by snatching her, Lucio had also snatched victory.

Unless they could stop him.

"Then it must have been Lucio's men," Derek

said. "There's a good chance that's where he's taken Sara."

Almost idly Kelsey said, "He won't expect you to come after her, will he?"

Andres looked surprised, then thoughtful. "No," he said slowly. "I suppose not. He would know I'd be cautious. Too great a chance of getting Sara . . . killed."

Raven kept her voice brisk, knowing what this waiting was doing to him. "All right. We have the advantage of surprise. We'll slip through the jungle and catch him off guard. Just us—none of your men."

"I can't ask—" Andres began.

"You aren't," she told him calmly. She met his steady gaze and smiled. "But we're going, all the same. Why else do you think we're here?"

His smile was crooked. "To help Sara."

"So? We're helping."

Mildly Zach said, "We even brought our own guns."

Lucio had gone to get the tape recorder. Sara took advantage of his absence and his man's still turned back. Flexing fingers that felt a little numb from loss of circulation, she leaned forward slowly, her eyes on that broad back, and reached into her right boot. The rope around her ankles wasn't very tight, which was a good thing; the short barrel of the derringer was wedged underneath it. She managed to get hold of it and ease it out.

She leaned back again, hiding the tiny gun as well as she could by raising her knees and by holding the gun against her thigh and covering it with her palm and fingers. And just in time, because Sabin turned around to leer at her. With an effort she ignored him.

The dizziness from the blow that had knocked her out and the later slap had faded somewhat, but she felt horribly shaky and sick. On the whole it was a good thing she was sitting with her back braced against the tree; she doubted she could have gotten to her feet, even if her ankles hadn't been tied.

With a detachment that came of having looked death in the face, Sara wondered if she could shoot both Lucio and Sabin without either returning the favor. It seemed doubtful. Lucio would likely be near enough for the derringer to have some effect, but Sabin, she thought, could probably withstand both barrels from a shotgun and keep coming.

Not a pleasant thought.

She looked up as Lucio approached, holding her face still with all her will. He was carrying a small portable tape recorder, and he set it on the table with the radio. Then he looked at Sabin and barked a short command, and Sara was so relieved that she almost sobbed aloud. He was sending the soldier away.

Probably to get the whip, she realized, relief vanishing in an instant. But the burly man disappeared into the thick undergrowth of the jungle.

"Where did you send him?" she asked.

Indifferently, clearly expecting nothing to come of it, Lucio said, "A short patrol around the perimeter."

"You don't think Andres will come after me," she noted.

Lucio smiled at her. "Certainly not. He knows that I would kill you instantly if he approached."

"Then he'd kill you."

With a shrug Lucio said, "I would have won."

His logic baffled her, and she stopped trying to make sense of it. She watched him adjust the recorder and move toward her. When he was still a few feet away, she got a good grip on the gun and raised her bound hands, the derringer pointed at him squarely. "Stop."

He did, but after a single incredulous glance at the tiny gun he laughed. "A child's toy!"

Evenly she said, "Deadly at close range. You're close enough. And I'm a good shot."

Lucio was still highly amused. "And assuming you managed to wound me with that little pop-gun? I'd still be able to draw my own gun."

"Not if I shoot you in the right place," she said grimly. "And I will."

"And then you will also shoot Sabin in the right place?"

"I'll worry about him when I have to." It occurred to her then that what she had ended up with was something of a standoff. She wanted the ropes untied but wasn't about to invite him close enough to do it. She couldn't get to her feet. Damn . . . damn . . . damn . . .

He took a half step toward her.

"Don't." Her gun was rock-steady. "Don't make me shoot you."

His unnaturally brilliant eyes were laughing at her. "You couldn't shoot a man," he said flatly and with utter certainty. "You won't. Nothing in your entire privileged life has prepared you to kill."

She thought of her parents lying in a pool of blood, thought of the last two years and her grim flight. She thought of the man she loved, his dream being choked to death by this evil man. She thought of Kadeira dying slowly.

"I can," she said. "I will."

Lucio laughed, took another half step.

"Don't—"

There was a sudden crash off to the right, the beginning of a warning shout cut off with chilling abruptness. Lucio's head turned, then turned back toward her in almost the same instant. With fury in his eyes he reached for his gun.

Sara pulled the trigger of the little derringer twice, instinctively rolling aside as he fell. She saw his face for an instant, saw the realization there. And she saw something else, though not what she'd expected to see. There was no snarl at death, no fury at having been beaten by the tool he'd meant to use against Andres. There was no grief or regret. What she saw on his face was . . .

Infinite surprise.

There was, Sara thought vaguely, a great deal of activity suddenly. And lots of people. She saw Josh Long and his wife Raven, as well as their friend Zach Steele. There was a big blond man with a hard face and strangely comforting eyes. There was another man, also big, with a pleasant face and rusty-colored hair. They all carried guns.

And there was Andres. He was just there, beside her, murmuring thickly in Spanish as he cut the ropes away and gathered her into his arms.

"You've been wounded," she said, worried.

He laughed, an odd sound. "A scratch," he said. "Nothing. Sara, my love, did he—"

"Didn't get the chance," she murmured, wincing as the circulation returned to her hands. She looked at the derringer she still held, wondering how she'd been able to fire it. Remarkable thing, the human will. Just remarkable. "I shot him, you know," she said.

"Yes," Andres said quietly. "You had no choice."

In an instant of clarity brought on by shock and exhaustion, Sara thought that she probably would have shot him, choice or no choice, but she didn't say it. Instead she rested her head on Andres's shoulder as he rose to his feet, holding her easily in his arms. "I hope you brought a jeep," she said idly. "It's a long way back to the house."

There was a husky feminine laugh nearby, and Sara saw Raven Long grin at Andres and say, "She'll do."

Sara smiled at her absently, then went to sleep.

She dreamed that Teo had kidnapped her again, because the same officious voice as before was saying such things as, "No concussion this time" and "Just bruises and shock."

She told the voice to go away and turned on her side without waking up.

Sara woke up finally, aware that hours had passed and that she was in Andres's bed—*their* bed, she amended. She woke up saying, "Ouch."

"That's the lip," Raven Long said sympathetically from her chair beside the bed. "Bruised and swollen, I'm afraid. Your cheek too."

Sara sat up, yawning carefully. She looked at the other woman. "Where's—"

"Andres? Downstairs talking to the guys. Josh and Derek have a business proposal for him, and since the doctor said you just needed sleep, I offered to take the vigil."

Sara blinked. "Thanks."

"Don't mention it."

Pushing the covers back, Sara saw that she was in her green nightgown. She looked at Raven.

"Andres," Raven said solemnly.

With equal gravity Sara said, "He always puts me in this gown when I'm unconscious." She sighed, then said, "Derek who?"

Raven didn't appear to find the question baffling. "Ross. The big blond man."

"Who's the other? Reddish hair, interesting smile?"

"Kelsey. You remember Zach, of course."

"Oh, of course. Um . . . who got Sabin?"

Raven lifted an inquiring brow.

"The soldier at Lucio's camp."

"Ah. Andres got him." Raven looked completely calm, but her eyes were watchful. "Unfortunately for Sabin."

Sara smiled a little. "Don't worry, I won't fall to pieces. If I hadn't killed Lucio, Andres would have. And Lucio was . . . was not a nice man." She half laughed at the understatement.

"If it helps, you did the world a service," Raven told her. "And you've walked through the fire. It didn't destroy you; it made you stronger. If, God forbid, you're faced with a similar situation, threats like his will never again have quite the power over you that they did the first time."

Sara thought about it. "I hope you're right. I don't ever want to feel that again."

"We came here partly to offer you a ride back to the States, you know," Raven said, perhaps changing the subject.

Or perhaps not. Sara smiled. "No. I belong here with Andres. But thank you."

Raven didn't try to dissuade her. Reflectively she said, "It won't be easy. It's a gamble living with such a man."

"You took the gamble."

"So I did. And do. Sometimes there just isn't a choice."

"Men of power," Sara said, thinking about it. "All of them downstairs—you could see it in their faces, their eyes. Maybe in different ways, but . . . men of power."

"Yes." Raven studied her. How different she was from their Sarah! Alike only in appearance. There was no serenity in this one, but there was a kind of calm—quiet and steely, like the eye of a hurricane. And better for her that way, Raven thought. She hadn't chosen a tame man or a tame life; her hard-won calm would serve them both well.

"I," Sara said suddenly, "am starving. I missed breakfast and lunch."

"Another hour," Raven said, "and you would have missed dinner too. Why don't you get changed while I go downstairs and interrupt affairs of state? The men also should be starving by now, and Maria said dinner would be ready at about this time."

Sara slid out of bed, noting that Raven remained unobtrusively close for those first shaky seconds, ready to lend a hand. The dizziness faded quickly, however. "I'm fine," Sara told her, cheerful to find that it was true.

Having come to the same conclusion herself, Raven said, "Great. Meet you downstairs, then."

Sara went along to her former room, where her clothing remained, and took a quick shower. She washed away the dirt and lingering stickiness of the jungle, and she washed away the regrets of having been forced to kill. It surprised her somewhat that those regrets should be so faint, and she considered it thoughtfully, realizing that she hadn't pulled the trigger in hate; she had done so with no other option available.

No choice. Her survival or his. And it wasn't important that she had hated and feared him, because those emotions hadn't prompted her to kill.

She accepted the facts, then promptly dismissed them.

Her reflection in the bathroom mirror had told her that Lucio's slap had done less damage than she'd expected. Half her face was sore and a bit puffy, and her lip was certainly swollen, but it didn't look too bad. She shrugged philosophically, wrapped her wet hair in a towel, and returned to the bedroom wearing a terry-cloth robe.

Andres was waiting for her. His expression eased when he saw her, his eyes brightening when she smiled and came to slide her arms around his waist. He had found time, she noted, to get cleaned up and changed, and the wound in his left arm seemed not to bother him at all, since he didn't hesitate to use the arm.

"I'm sorry," he said huskily after he kissed her.

Sara was surprised. "For what? It was my own

stupid fault, going out into the garden like that. And I should have been able to speak Spanish so I could have just called one of the men and told him about that gap in the fence."

"Still." He sighed, shook his head. "If it hadn't been for Josh and the others, I wouldn't even have dared to come after you."

Sara decided to change the subject. "What about the town, Andres?"

"Surprisingly little damage," he told her, watching with intent eyes as she went to the dresser and began dealing with her wet hair. "The people in the town joined my men, fighting Lucio's army. It was remarkable."

She smiled. "Expected, I would have thought." And before he could respond, she asked, "What about Lucio's army?"

"Most were captured. They're being held in the barracks."

"Not the prison?"

"No. I'll talk to them in a few days. Few are likely to be rabid revolutionaries. Most of them, I think, will choose to get on with their lives. We'll see."

Sara began changing into jeans and a knit top, very aware of Andres's steady gaze but disturbed only in the sensual sense. She wondered how early they could go to bed. "What about our guests?" she asked him.

"Josh's yacht is arriving here tomorrow," Andres said, his slightly rough voice indicating she wasn't the only one disturbed. "I've invited them to stay as long as they like."

"Good." She fastened her jeans and looked at him with unknowingly darkened eyes. "Um . . .

what about this business proposal of theirs? A good one?"

"Very good." He cleared his throat. "Josh and Derek want to invest in the island. They've worked out a plan, a schedule, so that the economy will benefit as soon as possible."

"A strong beginning," she noted with a smile.

"With luck."

"Luck is something you make. And you will."

Andres reached for her suddenly, pulling her into his arms. "I'm selfish," he murmured against her lips. "I want to make love to you right now, even after all you've been through. . . ."

"I slept for hours," she told him huskily, wreathing her arms around his neck, twining her fingers in the thick silk of his hair. "And I want you too. Now, right now."

"Our guests . . ."

"I think they'll understand," she said, coping with the buttons of his shirt. "I love you, darling. So much."

Andres lifted her, carried her to the bed. "If I lost you . . . *Dios*, I—"

"Never," she murmured, pulling his head down.

Nine

The house was quiet. Josh Long, his wife, and their friends had gone down to the harbor to meet the yacht that was due to arrive any time. Then they would all return to the house, where further plans would be made. The revolution—this one, at least—was over. It was time to begin rebuilding.

Andres would need her more than ever now, Sara knew that. She also knew that he was going to try to send her away. He had been badly shaken by Lucio's capture of her, and she knew the kind of hell he had gone through in the hours before she was safe again. She knew because she had gone through that as well.

The odd thing was that their reactions to that frightening span of hours were directly opposite—and yet each was showing the greatest strength possible. For Sara the strength came in the decision that she would remain; for Andres the strength came in the intention to send her away from him.

Sara knew it couldn't be avoided, knew they had to face this and put it behind them quickly. And so, when the others, escorted by Colonel Durant, had left for the harbor, she went into Andres's office. He was at his desk, going over the efficient paperwork that made up the "proposal" offered by Josh Long and Derek Ross. The proposal of aid to rebuild a torn country.

She went over to the window without speaking, gazing out at the deepening twilight. The room was in shadows; only his desk lamp was on. She knew he was watching her because she could feel his gaze; knew he was thinking of how to start this, of how to begin telling her he had to send her away. She could feel that too. And she wasn't surprised when the words he found belonged to a poet.

" 'You should have a softer pillow than my heart,' " he murmured suddenly.

"Byron." Sara drew a deep breath and turned away from the window. But she remained there, leaning back against the frame and gazing at him as he sat in a pool of light.

Andres half nodded. "Byron. And with one interpretation, true words for us. You should have a better life than I can offer, Sara." His voice was low, all the feeling squeezed out of it with a vise of control. "Even with Lucio gone, this will never be a safe place for you. I must steal what time I can, quickly, to try to build something lasting here, something good. But even with this help"—he gestured slightly at the papers before him— "the time may not be mine to steal. The risk to you . . ."

"I'm safe here," she said.

"He took you from me twice!" Andres said in a sudden fierceness.

"He's dead." She kept her voice quiet.

"Someone else will come. Someday." He made a rough sound that was half laugh but held no humor. "Someone always does. Hating, or seduced by a vision."

"Andres . . ."

"With me you'll never be safe." His voice was low, aching. "You'll be in danger as long as I live. I can't bear that, Sara. You must be safe, even if . . ."

"Even if it means leaving you?" Her face was in shadow; he couldn't see her expression.

"I won't put you in a cage!" he said intensely. "Iron bars, guards. I thought . . . I believed I could do that when I brought you back here. I believed I could love you enough so that you wouldn't see the bars or the guards. Or perhaps I believed you'd be generous in your own love and that you could ignore the cage. But I haven't the right to ask that of you."

"You have the right."

"No. No man has the right to build a cage around the woman he loves. For any reason. You must be free. And you must be safe. Nothing else matters."

"Free? What does that mean, Andres?"

He hesitated, then said roughly, "You know what it means."

"Free to come and go?"

"Yes."

She let the silence build, then said quietly, "You want to send me away, and apparently I'm free to go. You won't be warning off visitors any longer, so it seems clear I'd be free to return. That sounds like freedom to me."

He shook his head a little. "Sara, outside these gates you'd always be escorted by armed guards. That isn't freedom."

"Depends," she said softly, "on my definition of freedom, doesn't it? And my definition happens to include loving you and being with you. Iron bars don't make a cage, Andres. Guards don't make a cage. Those things happen to be a part of your life, and now they're a part of mine. They don't matter."

"Your safety does," he said, his voice strained. "And not even the guards and the bars can keep you safe."

"If they can't," she said, "nothing can."

He was silent, something stricken in his eyes.

"Andres . . ." Her voice softened. "Sending me away won't keep me safe. You must know that. I could walk down Main Street, U.S.A., and some crackpot with a gun could decide on a little target practice. I could crash in a car or plane, get run over in the street. I could fall down stairs. I could get sick."

"You're a target here. Because of me you're a target."

"And I'm a danger to you. A weapon to use against you."

He gestured slightly, impatiently. "That isn't important."

"Isn't it?" Calmly she said, "If I knew for *certain* that my leaving Kadeira would keep you safe, I'd go. But it wouldn't, because your life will always be dangerous. And if you knew for *certain* that sending me away would keep me safe, you would have done it days ago."

"Sara—"

"I'm not leaving. I'll take the risk."

"The risk is too great!"

"No. Like all risks in life, it's a question of degree. I weighed all the risks against my dream. And the dream won."

Her admission surprised him. Frowning a little, he rose from his chair and came slowly toward her, needing to see her face now. She didn't move, didn't meet him halfway. She simply waited. When he stood an arm's length away, he saw that her face was as calm as her voice, that her eyes were steady.

"What dream?" he asked after a moment.

She smiled, a sudden glimmer of amusement in her eyes. "I'm afraid I haven't had time to have my dream painted. But one day I will."

He was puzzled, intent, some of the tension draining from his face and posture. "Sara, what are you talking about?"

Her smiled remained. "My dream. I have one, too, you know. A dream of living with the only man I've ever loved. Of helping him make his country whole again. A dream of waking up in his arms every morning, of seeing his smile and hearing his voice. A dream of having his children." She drew a deep breath. "I weighed that against the dangers—and the dangers never had a chance."

In the instant before he pulled her into his arms, Sara knew without a doubt that she had won.

It was a long moment before Andres could speak, and when he did, his voice was unsteady. "It won't be easy, my love. Until things improve on Kadeira, a spark could set off another war. And there's so much to do."

Sara pulled back just far enough to smile up at him. "I know. And *you* should know that I don't intend just to knit and weed the roses. I have a business degree with a minor in economics. I can help." She waited, watched while he accepted that she wouldn't wait safely inside this house but would be actively working for the good of Kadeira. For his dream as well as hers.

Andres smiled, his eyes glowing. "I believed you were strong, *mi corazón*. It seems I was right."

The sounds of arrival were heard at the front door.

Sara stood on tiptoe to kiss him. "You certainly were."

Then they went to greet the visitors and to set about healing a wounded country.

Epilogue

He was a rotund little man, an unashamed paunch straining the seams of his tailored vest. Shiny wing-tipped shoes were on his small feet. He had a great leonine head with a cherub's face, small brightly twinkling eyes, and pouty lips. And he was so much a caricature of a strutting bantam rooster pleased with his own importance that few people whom he would encounter casually would even look for more than that.

There were those who knew better. A relative few, certainly, but those who had learned their lesson had learned it well. And they knew that the man who called himself Hagen was as harmless as a battleship, as innocent as a shark in bloody waters, as foolish and inconsequential as a hydrogen bomb. They knew, in fact, that he possessed a Machiavellian mind of frightening ruthlessness, an absolute vision of justice, and an inability to give up even when the cause seemed lost.

Recently he had also developed a somewhat unwelcome ability as matchmaker, but that was neither here nor there, he had told himself.

On this fine morning Hagen sat alone in his office. Atop his spotless desk reposed a chessboard. On the black side, all the pieces except the king had been taken off the board; on the white side, the king and queen, bishops, rooks, and knights were ranged neatly. There were no pawns, which was rather deceptive, since Hagen tended to think of all people as mere pawns.

And Hagen was planning.

He studied the board for a few minutes, pudgy hands clasped and at least two chins resting on them. His small twinkling eyes moved back and forth between the kings thoughtfully. Black and white. The black king alone; the white king with a small army around him. "Small" being, of course, a relative term.

Hagen eyed the rooks and bishops and knights. He especially eyed the white queen. The most powerful piece on the board, the queen. And in this case, certainly . . .

He reached out and slowly picked up the white king. He held it in his hand for a moment before closing his fingers around it gently. He looked back at the board. The space beside the white queen looked very empty, indeed.

Hagen might have felt a moment's compunction then. Some uneasiness certainly sent a spasm across his cherubic face and tightened his pouty lips. It was a fleeting thing, swiftly over. In his mind he watched the white pieces move in various ways toward the black king. Feints, all-out attacks. He watched them fiercely protecting their white queen.

And they would, of course.

"Pandora's box," he muttered aloud. He wasn't altogether certain he was prepared to open it. But what choice did he have? Plans so carefully laid couldn't be easily discarded. Not his plans, at any rate. And he'd already set them in motion. They would take time, of course, to execute, and he would have to be extremely careful.

The minor feints he had arranged these last months had shown clearly that the white king's security was impressive. Quite impressive, in fact. Response time to any threat had been the fastest he'd seen. But there were weaknesses in that apparently impenetrable armor. Chinks.

A great deal, he thought, could fall through very small chinks.

As an intellectual and tactical exercise, it was going to be interesting. He had the uneasy feeling, however, that his own physical safety might be endangered this time. Some people, he thought, seemed unconvinced that the end always justified the means.

Still.

Pandora's box. "The ills of mankind," he said aloud, then shook his head. No, not that, perhaps. But furies, certainly. Strong furies, as he had cause to know. He shook his head again and set the white king gently to one side of the board.

No choice.

He was a rotund little man, comical in appearance but not in reality. Not comical. He was dangerous. Even those few who knew appearances deceived didn't know quite how true that was in relation to him. They would learn.

If they survived the lesson.

THE EDITOR'S CORNER

Have you been having fun with our **HOMETOWN HUNK CONTEST**? If not, hurry and join in the excitement by entering a gorgeous local man to be a LOVESWEPT cover hero. The deadline for entries is September 15, 1988, and contest rules are in the back of our books. Now, if you need some inspiration, we have six incredible hunks in our LOVESWEPTs this month . . . and you can dream about the six to come next month . . . to get you in the mood to discover one of your own.

First next month, there's Jake Kramer, "danger in the flesh," the fire fighter hero of new author Terry Lawrence's **WHERE THERE'S SMOKE, THERE'S FIRE,** LOVESWEPT #288. When Jennie Cisco sets eyes on Jake, she knows she's in deep trouble—not so much because of the fire he warns her is racing out of control toward her California retreat, as because of the man himself. He is one tough, yet tender, and decidedly sexy man . . . and Jennie isn't the least bit prepared for his steady and potent assault on her senses and her soul. A musician who can no longer perform, Jenny has secluded herself in the mountains. She fiercely resists Jake's advances . . . until she learns that it may be more terrifying to risk losing him than to risk loving him. A romance that blazes with passion!

Our next hunk-of-the-month, pediatrician Patrick Hunter, will make you laugh along with heroine Megan Murphy as he irresistibly attracts her in **THANKS-GIVING,** LOVESWEPT #289, by Janet Evanovich. In this absolutely delightful romance set in Williamsburg, Virginia, at turkey time, Megan and Dr. Pat suddenly find themselves thrown together as the temporary parents of an abandoned baby. Wildly attracted to each

(continued)

other, both yearn to turn their "playing house" into the real thing, yet circumstances *and* Megan's past conspire to keep them apart . . . until she learns that only the doctor who kissed her breathless can heal her lonely heart. A love story as full of chuckles as it is replete with the thrills of falling in love.

Move over Crocodile Dundee, because we've got an Aussie hero to knock the socks off any woman! Brig McKay is a hell-raiser, to be sure, and one of the most devastatingly handsome men ever to cross the path of Deputy Sheriff Millie Surprise, in LOVESWEPT #290, **CAUGHT BY SURPRISE,** by Deborah Smith. Brig has to do some time in Millie's jail, and after getting to know the petite and feisty officer, he's determined to make it a life sentence! But in the past Millie proved to be too much for the men in her life to take, and she's sure she'll turn out to be an embarrassment to Brig. You'll delight in the rollicking, exciting, merry chase as Brig sets out to capture his lady for all time. A delight!

You met that good-looking devil Jared Loring this month, and next Joan Elliott Pickart gives you his own beguiling love story in **MAN OF THE NIGHT,** LOVESWEPT #291. Tabor O'Casey needed Jared's help to rescue her brother, who'd vanished on a mysterious mission, and so she'd called on this complicated and enigmatic man who'd befriended her father. Jared discovers he can refuse her nothing. Though falling as hard and fast for Tabor as she is falling for him, Jared suspects her feelings. And, even in the midst of desperate danger, Tabor must pit herself against the shadowed soul of this man and dare to prove him wrong about her love. A breathlessly beautiful romance!

Here is inspirational hunk #5: Stone Hamilton, one glorious green-eyed, broad-shouldered man and the hero of **TIME OUT**, LOVESWEPT #292, by Patt

(continued)

Bucheister. Never have two people been so mismatched as Stone and beautiful Whitney Grant. He's an efficiency expert; she doesn't even own a watch. He's supremely well-organized, call him Mr. Order; she's delightfully scattered, call her Miss Creativity. Each knows that something *has* to give as they are drawn inexorably into a love affair as hot as it is undeniable. Just how these two charming opposites come to resolve their conflicts will make for marvelous reading next month.

Would you believe charismatic, brawny, handsome, *and* rich? Well, that's just what hero Sam Garrett is! You'll relish his all-out efforts to capture the beautiful and winsome Max Strahan, in **WATER WITCH**, LOVE-SWEPT #293, by Jan Hudson. Hired to find water on a rocky Texas ranch, geologist Max doesn't want anyone to know her methods have nothing to do with science—and everything to do with the mystical talent of using a dowsing stick. Sam's totally pragmatic—except when it comes to loving Max, whose pride and independence are at war with her reckless desire for the man she fears will laugh at her "gift." Then magic, hot and sweet, takes over and sets this glorious romance to simmering! A must-read love story.

Enjoy all the hunks this month and every month!

Carolyn Nichols

Carolyn Nichols
  Editor
LOVESWEPT
Bantam Books
666 Fifth Avenue
New York, NY 10103

NEW!

Handsome Book Covers Specially Designed To Fit Loveswept Books

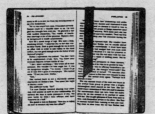

Our new French Calf Vinyl book covers come in a set of three great colors—royal blue, scarlet red and kachina green.

Each 7" × 9½" book cover has two deep vertical pockets, a handy sewn-in bookmark, and is soil and scratch resistant.

To order your set, use the form below.

THE DELANEY DYNASTY

Men and women whose loves and passions are so glorious it takes many great romance novels by three bestselling authors to tell their tempestuous stories.

THE SHAMROCK TRINITY

☐ 21786 RAFE, THE MAVERICK
   by Kay Hooper $2.75
☐ 21787 YORK, THE RENEGADE
   by Iris Johansen $2.75
☐ 21788 BURKE, THE KINGPIN
   by Fayrene Preston $2.75

THE DELANEYS OF KILLAROO

☐ 21872 ADELAIDE, THE ENCHANTRESS
   by Kay Hooper $2.75
☐ 21873 MATILDA, THE ADVENTURESS
   by Iris Johansen $2.75
☐ 21874 SYDNEY, THE TEMPTRESS
   by Fayrene Preston $2.75

☐ 26991 THIS FIERCE SPLENDOR
   by Iris Johansen $3.95

Now Available!
THE DELANEYS: *The Untamed Years*

☐ 21897 GOLDEN FLAMES *by Kay Hooper* $3.50
☐ 21898 WILD SILVER *by Iris Johansen* $3.50
☐ 21999 COPPER FIRE *by Fayrene Preston* $3.50

Buy these books at your local bookstore or use this page to order:

- -

Bantam Books, Dept. SW7, 414 East Golf Road, Des Plaines, IL 60016

Please send me the books I have checked above. I am enclosing $_____
(please add $2.00 to cover postage and handling). Send check or money order—no cash or C.O.D.s please.

Mr/Ms _____

Address _____

City/State _____ Zip _____

SW7—10/88

Please allow four to six weeks for delivery. This offer expires 4/89.
Prices and availability subject to change without notice.

Special Offer
Buy a Bantam Book
for only 50¢.

Now you can have Bantam's catalog filled with hundreds of titles plus take advantage of our unique and exciting bonus book offer. A special offer which gives you the opportunity to purchase a Bantam book for only 50¢. Here's how!

By ordering any five books at the regular price per order, you can also choose any other single book listed (up to a $5.95 value) for just 50¢. Some restrictions do apply, but for further details why not send for Bantam's catalog of titles today!

Just send us your name and address and we will send you a catalog!